The Secret Lives of Baltimore Girls 2

The Secret Lives of Baltimore Girls 2

Katt

www.urbanbooks.net

Urban Books, LLC
300 Farmingdale Road, NY-Route 109
Farmingdale, NY 11735

The Secret Lives of Baltimore Girls 2
Copyright © 2020 Katt

All rights reserved. No part of this book may be repro-
duced in any form or by any means without prior consent
of the Publisher, except brief quotes used in reviews.

ISBN 13: 978-1-64556-020-3
ISBN 10: 1-64556-020-1

First Trade Paperback Printing June 2020
Printed in the United States of America

10 9 8 7 6 5 4 3 2 1

*This is a work of fiction. Any references or similarities
to actual events, real people, living or dead, or to real
locales are intended to give the novel a sense of reality.
Any similarity in other names, characters, places, and
incidents is entirely coincidental.*

Distributed by Kensington Publishing Corp.
Submit Orders to:
Customer Service
400 Hahn Road
Westminster, MD 21157-4627
Phone: 1-800-733-3000
Fax: 1-800-659-2436

The Secret Lives of Baltimore Girls 2

by

Katt

Prologue

"Hello?" Mikayla's weak voice called out.

She had felt no terror in life like the one of waking up with a cloth bag over her head. It was proving hard to recall the past hour of her life. The last thing she remembered was being at the launch of Charlie's clothing line; the next, she was waking up bound to a chair.

"Mikayla? I–is that you?"

"Charlie." Mikayla sighed, recognizing her friend's voice. "What's happening? I can't see or move."

"Me either," Charlie said. "Is this some sort of sick joke? I–I can't remember anything."

"H–hey, what's going on?" A third voice joined the conversation.

It was a little drowsy, but Mikayla would know her good friend's voice anywhere.

"Emerson?"

"Yes." Emerson sounded a little more awake this time. "Why am I tied to a chair, and what is this over my head? It smells terrible. Charlie, is this your idea of a joke?"

"It wasn't me. I swear!" Charlie exclaimed. "I don't know what's going on."

The hairs on the back of Mikayla's neck were standing up, and there was a chill going down her spine. She could hear Emerson and Charlie going back and forth, but she could hear someone else breathing in the room behind her—directly behind her. She sucked in her breath and held it, hoping that whatever was happening was just a prank gone too far. But when she felt pressure on her temple and heard the sound of a gun cocking, she knew it wasn't a prank.

"Give me one good reason not to kill you right now." A deep baritone voice erupted in the darkness.

"Who was that?" Charlie asked. "Was that a gun I just heard?"

"Yes. He has it to my head," Mikayla said in a barely audible whisper.

"Listen, whoever you are, I have a lot of money. I can give you whatever it is that you want. You don't have to hurt anybody here today," Emerson said, trying to reason with him.

"Ain't this something. The crazy bitch is trying to bribe me," the man said crudely. "I don't want your money. What I want only she can give to me. Isn't that right, Mikayla?"

Mikayla tried to steady her breathing. She would recognize the way he spat her name anywhere. "Damian?"

"In the flesh," he said.

"But why? I did everything you asked!"

"Damian, as in your crazy-ass brother Damian?" Emerson asked with slight panic in her voice. "He's the one who put these things over our faces?"

Damian pulled the bag off Emerson's head. "Maybe the bags were a little over the top. I just didn't want you waking up on our way here."

"Here? Where are we?" Mikayla asked.

"Let me help you out," he said and took the bag from over her head.

Mikayla blinked quickly as she tried to adjust to the light in the room, and when she focused, she was taken aback. They were in her house, in her basement, tied to the chairs that went to her new stained wood table. She tried to wiggle her wrists, but they were wrapped tight.

The women looked at each other, sitting in a circle, still dressed in their evening attire with frightened expressions on their faces. Mikayla tried to reach out to give her friends a hug, but she couldn't. Her hands were bound to the chair.

Charlie's face went from scared to angry as the reality of the situation set in. "What the fuck do you think you're doing?" she asked. "My fiancé is going to throw you back in jail, you greasy motherfucker!"

"You talk a good game, Charlie, but I think you forgot that you're the one tied to a chair, and I'm the one with the gun." Damian smirked and shook his pistol at her. "Also, nobody knows where you are. They think the three of you went to celebrate."

"Whatever you're planning to do, you won't get away with it." Charlie tried to say it with confidence, but her shaky voice gave her away.

"What *is* it that I'm trying to get away with, Charlie?" Damian asked and walked up on her. He leaned his face so close to hers that when she turned her head, his lips brushed against her cheek. "Why don't you just ask what you really want to know?"

"Are . . . are you going to kill us?"

"Well, that depends on Mikayla," Damian said and smiled at his sister. "If she's willing to cooperate, I'm willing to let all of you walk out of here with your lives."

"Cooperate with what?" Emerson asked and looked at Mikayla. "What is he talking about?"

"He wants me to tell the truth," Mikayla whispered.

"Tell the truth about what?" Emerson furrowed her brow at her friend.

Damian left Charlie, knelt in front of Mikayla, and smiled sinisterly in her face.

"Yeah, tell the truth about what, Mikayla?" he mocked.

"Why now?" Mikayla asked, ignoring the question. "After all this time, why now? I've done everything you asked me to do. You and Jewel were supposed to be out of my life!"

"We were family, Mikayla. Or at least I thought we were. You took me from my mother's home and put me in the position to go to jail. Do you know what it feels like to have nobody care about you?"

"I kept money on your books."

"That doesn't make up for the fact that you weren't there. You turned your back on me. The only person who was there for me was Mama. After all the damage that you caused, the truth still refuses to come from your lips," Damian said, stepping back and pointing his gun at her. "One thing I learned when I was locked down is that sometimes you have to apologize to yourself for something somebody else did. This isn't going to be one of those times. I think shooting one of your fingers off will be the perfect motivation."

Emerson and Charlie screamed as Damian's finger got tighter around the trigger.

Right before a shot rang out, the door to the basement opened. Mikayla had forgotten she'd told Charles, her soon-to-be-ex-husband, he could come by after the event to grab some of his things. Mikayla had never been so happy to see him.

There was a shocked expression on his face as he saw the scene taking place. He stepped off the last stair and looked at the gun in Damian's hand.

"Charles, call the police! My brother is trying to kill me!" Mikayla cried.

Damian turned his gaze to Charles, who shook his head.

"Damian, I told you to make sure she was dead before I got here and to make it look like a burglar did it," Charles

said, sending Mikayla's heart to her stomach. "And what the hell are her friends doing here? Now we have to kill them all."

"Charles . . ." Mikayla's voice faded.

She took in his appearance and saw that he was dressed in work attire. His tailored suit was fitted over his new gym body, and his diamond cufflinks flashed whenever he moved. He glowered down at her like she was the most disgusting thing he had ever seen in his life.

"Don't look at me like that. I hate you, and you know that," he told her. "With you gone, not only will I get my house and my girls back, but there's also the five hundred thousand life insurance policy I get if you die."

Emerson started to scream at the top of her lungs, and to shut her up, Damian backhanded her so hard he busted her lip.

"Beating up women. Is that the kind of man you are?" Mikayla spat.

"I'll do something better. You failed at saving your friends, so now you get to watch them die," Damian said. He cocked his gun and pointed it at Emerson's bleeding face. "Three. Two—"

"Okay! I'll tell the truth," Mikayla screamed through her tears. "I'll tell the truth. I did it!"

"Did *what*?"

"I killed him. I'm the one who killed him!"

"Killed who, Kay Kay?" Charlie asked in a tone barely above a whisper.

"Our foster father," Mikayla said, sobbing. "The murder Damian went to jail for. I'm the one who pulled the trigger. I'm so sorry. We were so young. I didn't think they would sentence you to all that time. You gave up your life for me."

"Finally. That's the first time you've been real with yourself in years, isn't it, sis? I did all that time for a crime I didn't even do, and you couldn't even visit me. And you keep taking from me. I should have snapped your neck the moment I saw you when I first got out, but I didn't. That was my mistake."

"I said what you wanted me to say. Now, can't you just let us go? Like you said you would."

"I'm happy that you finally admitted what you did to me. I just wanted to see if you would tell the truth. But I'm not here for that. I'm here because you have something I want. Where is it?"

"W–what?" Mikayla asked between sobs.

"You know exactly what I'm talking about. You thought I wasn't going to find out? Now, you have a chance to save your friends. Tell me what you did with it. You have five seconds."

Mikayla's eyes were on the gun Damian now had pointed at her friend's chest as he counted down. Her lips opened and closed like she wanted to say something, but she couldn't get it out. Charlie and Emerson were crying loudly, but that was just background noise to Mikayla.

"One," Damian said.

"No!" Mikayla screamed.

But he didn't care. That time, Damian didn't hesitate to pull the trigger.

The events of the two months leading up to that night flashed before Mikayla's eyes, and she wondered in the final moments of her life if anything could have been done to lead to a different fate.

Chapter 1

Mikayla

Two Months Earlier

"Girls, what did I tell you both about leaving your socks just laying everywhere around the house?" Mikayla groaned as she almost walked by a sock wedged between the living room couch and the wall behind it. She didn't know what in the world her daughters, Zuri and Kai, did when she was upstairs in her room working on her women's empowerment blog, but she was always finding things in the strangest places. The other day, she'd found socks in the toilet, and of course nobody could tell her what that was about.

"Sorry, Mom!" Zuri, the oldest daughter, said, rushing down the stairs of their two-story home.

Mikayla didn't even have to point the sock out for Zuri to know exactly where it was. Mikayla shook her head. She just couldn't believe how big they'd gotten right before her eyes.

Zuri snatched the sock and exited the living room as quickly as she came. Mikayla was sure she was going to hole herself up in her room and gossip to her best friend on the new cell phone Mikayla had just gotten her.

Almost two years had passed since she'd separated from their father, Charles, and Zuri was now in the sixth grade. Kai was right behind her in the fourth. They'd grown accustomed to a one-parent household, especially since they went to stay with their father every other weekend. It was an arrangement that Mikayla was okay with, especially since communication between her and Charles was kept at a bare minimum. What she wasn't okay with, however, was the fact that Charles still hadn't signed the divorce papers. He argued that Mikayla didn't have anything when she came into the wedding, so she should leave with nothing more than the house and child support. Mikayla's legal fees were eating away at the money she did have, and she had no choice but to find a way to make some or she would be broke. However, she wanted to do something she wanted to do. She had been an ant under Charles's thumb for too long, and she was ready to reclaim her identity.

At the time, all she wanted to do was help women who were, or had been, in the same shoes as her. The women in the world who felt helpless and unheard. She wanted to give them a voice. So, she started a blog called The Sisterhood. It was a safe place for women to express themselves and help each other overcome obstacles of being survivors of any kind of abuse. And thank God for her girl Emerson. All it took was a few retweets and IG posts to her hundreds of thousands of followers to get Mikayla on the right start. Before she knew it, The Sisterhood had grown from more than just an online blog. Soon Mikayla was getting booked to give motivational speeches and even go on talk shows.

It all came so fast, but Mikayla had finally found her calling. She wasn't built to be somebody's wife and personal masturbation device. She had a place in the world, helping people. Sometimes Damian crossed her mind, and although she hadn't seen him or her mother recently, she knew they would be back sooner or later. But when she saw her brother again, she hoped that maybe she could help him.

Mikayla put her hands on her hips and gave her clean home a once over to make sure there was nothing else out of place before she, too, disappeared in her room for the evening. The universe had other plans for her, however. As soon as she turned in the direction of the staircase, the doorbell sounded.

"It's almost eight thirty at night," she said, checking the gold watch on her wrist as she headed over to the door. "Who could be here?"

She peered through the peephole to see who her guest was and smacked her lips before opening the door.

"Dang, girl, it took you long enough!" Charlie said, bursting through the door with her son in her arms. "Here, hold MJ for me, please. I have to pee so bad! I was at the fabric store not too far from here, and I was going to try to make it home, but—"

"You didn't make it," Mikayla said, taking MJ from Charlie. "Go pee, girl. I'll keep my nephew company. Isn't that right, Man?" Mikayla called him by his nickname and kissed his chunky cheeks.

He was the cutest toddler with his caramel complexion and deep dimples. He was the perfect mixture of Charlie and her boyfriend, Mason. His eyes were wide like Charlie's, and he had eyelashes so long they could make a woman jealous. He smiled at Mikayla before resting his head on her chest.

"Oh, my baby is tired. Poor baby, and your mama got you out and about," she cooed down at him and ran her hands tenderly over his soft curls.

"Zuri!" Mikayla called out.

"Yes, Mommy?" Zuri said when she came back down the stairs. Her eyes lit up when she saw who was in her mother's arms. "MJ!"

"Here, take his coat off and carry him upstairs with you and your sister so I can chat with Auntie Charlie for a bit, okay?"

"Okay," Zuri said and whisked MJ back upstairs with her.

When they were gone, Mikayla went into the kitchen and poured two glasses of wine. She placed them down on the high-top dining room table and sat down, waiting for her friend.

She'd just taken a sip from her glass when Charlie rounded the hallway corner. She draped her burnt orange peacoat over the back of her chair at the table and sat down across from Mikayla. She was glowing, and the sight of it made Mikayla more than happy. She, Charlie, and Emerson tried to hit the gym together twice a week so all of their bodies looked good, but there was something else making Charlie look so great. Love. It was apparent by the way she walked that Mason was making her a happy woman.

Mikayla was glad that the two of them could live their happily ever after in peace. She had to admit it was weird at first seeing the two of them together—especially since Mason was Emerson's ex-husband and they had been together for so long. But just like everything else, it was simply another hurdle to get over. It took Emerson some time to fully come around to the idea, but now she and MJ were almost inseparable.

"Whew, girl! I had to go *bad*!" Charlie said, fanning herself.

"Obviously. Especially since you're popping up like this on a school night," Mikayla responded with a raised eyebrow.

"Girl, who are you fooling? Those girls do not be 'sleep by nobody's nine o'clock."

"And how would you know?"

"Because Zuri called me last night at ten and asked me for my Netflix password," Charlie answered matter-of factly, then realized she'd said too much. "I mean, that might not have been Zuri."

"Uh-huh!" Mikayla said with a laugh. "Now I know I'm going to have to confiscate phones at bedtime."

"Don't do that to my baby," Charlie said, giggling. "You're going to get my titi privileges taken away."

"Titi privileges?"

"Yeah, you know when your nieces come and tell you stuff that they can't tell their mom," Charlie said with a shrug. "So that we can, of course, tell their mom later."

"Good save," Mikayla said, lifting her glass.

"Always." Charlie lifted her glass too, and they both took a few sips of wine.

"Have you talked to Em?" Charlie asked.

"Not since this morning. Why?"

"No reason. I've just been calling her since earlier, and she hasn't answered the phone."

"Oh, really? That's weird," Mikayla said and looked away quickly.

The gesture didn't go unnoticed by Charlie, who pointed her finger at Mikayla's face. "You know something!"

"I have no idea what you're talking about."

"Like hell you don't. Spill it!" Charlie coaxed.

"She asked me not to say anything."

"Under the pretenses that you would tell me anyway so that she wouldn't have to tell me."

"What?" Mikayla made a face at her friend's logic.

"Come onnnnn, Kay Kay! Wait!" Charlie's mouth formed an *O*, and she gasped. "She got a man, didn't she?"

Mikayla's smile said it all, and Charlie screamed.

"Oh my God! She has a man? And she felt like she couldn't tell me?"

"In all fairness, the only reason I found out was because I ran into the two of them at the grocery store."

"They're grocery shopping together?" Charlie asked incredulously. "Oh, this is serious then."

"That's what I said!" Mikayla explained, feeling herself growing excited. She finally had someone to talk about this exciting news. "And girl, he's *fine*."

"I heard the hell out of that. It's about time since, well . . ."

"Since you stole her man?" Mikayla joked and instantly saw Charlie get tense. "Girl, I am just playing with you. We both know that Emerson and Mason were done way before you two got together. But still, it's nice to see her finally jump back out there since her last dating scandal. That crap with Macy was just a mess."

"True," Charlie said and shuddered slightly. "Anyways, I'm glad our friend finally has a boo. And if not anything else, I just hope she has somebody who can knock the dust out that pussy."

Mikayla choked on her wine. "Charlie!"

"What? I'm just saying. It's been a while," Charlie said with a knowing look. "Speaking of men, how have you been? Charles been giving you any trouble lately?"

"Besides trying to reason with me about this divorce? Nope."

"How's that going?"

"Well, if what my lawyer tells me is true, I'll be getting half of everything plus a hefty amount in monthly child support until the girls are eighteen."

"Good!" Charlie beamed but noticed the sad expression on Mikayla's face. "Or not good? What's wrong, Kay Kay?"

"I don't know. I mean, I just never imagined my marriage going to shit like this. And as far as the money I'm going to get, Charles is right. I didn't work to earn any of it."

"Oh, no you don't!"

"No I don't what, girl?"

"Pulling that 'I feel sorry for Charles' crap. That man beat you and secluded you for *years*. I can't even begin to imagine the hell you endured while being under the same roof as him, but because of it, you earned every penny. If I was the judge, I would give you everything. An evil man like that doesn't even deserve a pot to piss in."

"You're right."

"I know I'm right," Charlie said, downing the rest of her glass.

"Whatever. How are things between you and Mason?"

"That man is an angel sent from God, Kay Kay. I tell you, he is so good to me and his son it almost makes no sense," Charlie said quickly. "The other day, I came home to a trail of rose petals leading to the bedroom, and he was sitting on the bed with a box of chocolates over his—well, you know. It was beautiful. I love him."

"I can tell you do," Mikayla said with a smile. "You deserve it too. MJ looked like he's getting big, too!"

"He's almost in a size four. Can you believe it?"

"Gotta stop feeding him."

"Shoot, if everything goes as planned with this clothing business, I'll make his clothes myself," Charlie beamed.

"I don't think my nephew wants to wear tailored suits all the time, Charlie." Mikayla giggled.

"Well, he might not have a choice," Charlie said with a grin. She got up and put her coat on. "Well, baby, let me get out of here. I need to get home to my man before he sends a patrol car looking for me."

"And we both know he will." Mikayla stood up and gave Charlie a hug. "Maybe sometime this week the three of us can get some coffee after the gym and catch up?"

"Sounds like a plan to me." Charlie released her and bounded up the stairs to get MJ.

When she came down, she was holding a sleeping toddler in her arms. "I don't know what those girls of yours do to my son, but they knock him out every time. I'll call you tomorrow."

Mikayla walked Charlie to the door and watched them safely get into the car and pull off before she shut and locked her door. She cleared the dining room table and rinsed out the wine glasses before turning off the lights to kitchen. She was about to go upstairs when she realized she had forgotten one thing. Mikayla walked toward the wall alarm by the garage door to set it.

Chapter 2

Charlie

She didn't want to leave Mikayla's house as quickly as she had. After all, they hadn't seen each other in a little while. But the longer Charlie stayed, the longer she had to lie to her friend's face. She glanced in the rearview mirror and smiled at the sight of her son sleeping so peacefully in his car seat.

She might have been a little biased, but she thought that he was the most handsome baby boy in the world. She loved him to pieces and was thankful to be his mother, which was why it pained her to feel things falling apart with his father. She didn't know what was happening between her and Mason, but it was something. A bad something. She barely saw him with his new work schedule. When he *was* home, he spent time with MJ and then disappeared inside of the bedroom for the rest of the night. Their lovemaking was almost nonexistent, and Charlie was even starting to question if Mason was still attracted to her. She knew for a moment she gained a few extra pounds after having the baby, but now her body was back snatched. Still, she knew it took more than having a good body to keep a man. If his heart wasn't in it anymore, it didn't matter what she looked like.

Charlie sighed when she pulled into the driveway of the home she shared with Mason. It was a house, but it wasn't her dream house. When Mason showed her the house for the first time, she decided to focus on the positive aspects of the situation.

"So, what do you think?" Mason asked, standing in the living room.

Charlie, not wanting to hurt his feelings, said, "I love it."

"I knew you would. The moment I saw it, I said to myself, 'This house is the perfect place for my family.' MJ will have his own bedroom and playroom."

Charlie smiled. It was true that MJ would have plenty of room, but that didn't make up for the small kitchen and the bathrooms that needed an update. Charlie went along with it, figuring that they would rent for a few years, then save enough to buy their own dream home.

But now, all Charlie could feel was him distancing himself. She got herself and MJ out of the car and hurried in the cold toward the front door. Before she reached it, it swung open, and she was happy that she didn't have to dig in her purse to find her keys.

"Thank you," she said, smiling when she saw Mason standing behind the door in his pajamas. "I didn't think you'd still be up."

"I was waiting for you and Little Man to get home. Here, let me help you," he said and took MJ from her. "Wow, he's really getting heavy."

"Tell me about it," Charlie said, shutting and locking the door behind her. "I don't know what it is we've been feeding that boy, but he's solid."

"Like his old man," Mason said. "I'm gonna go lay him down. There's something I want to talk to you about. I'll be right back."

Charlie sat in the living room, waiting for Mason to finish with MJ. She wondered what he wanted to talk about. She had a bad feeling, and her stomach was churning with nerves. She leaned back on her soft black couch and inhaled the sweet aroma of the vanilla-scented candle burning, hoping it would calm her down.

She closed her eyes for a moment but opened them when she felt her shoe slide off. Mason had come back downstairs and was setting one of her boots to the side. He had her feet in his lap and smiled at her before he removed the other shoe.

"What are you doing?" Charlie asked.

"About to rub my woman's feet. What does it look like I'm doing?"

"Oh, is that right?" she asked and adjusted herself on the couch. "Well, I'm not going to pass on a good foot rub."

Mason's hands were so strong and warm that Charlie instantly felt her body relax. He worked his thumbs over every nook and cranny like a professional. A moan slipped from Charlie's lips, and she didn't even care.

"I know it's been feeling like I've been neglecting you, and I apologize for that," he said in a sensual, low tone. His eyes were on Charlie's, and there was a genuine expression on his face. "I sometimes have to remind myself that the most important piece of me is you."

Charlie was relieved to hear these words. They were exactly what she needed.

"Why have you been distant lately? Are you not attracted to me anymore?"

"Are you crazy?" Mason asked and looked at Charlie as if she were really crazy. "Have you seen yourself lately?"

"Then what is it? Is there somebody else?"

"Now you really sound crazy." Mason let go of her foot and scooted closer to her. "Charlie, there is nobody else. Now, I will admit that my hours at work may get a little strenuous, but you gotta know that I love you and would never step out on this family. My caseload has been stacked lately. I don't know what's going on in this city, but the crime rate is soaring, and we're short a detective, so I've had to take on extra cases. Okay?"

"Okay." Charlie kissed him.

"What was that?" he asked when she pulled away.

"A kiss."

"Was it? That didn't feel like the kiss of a woman who wants some dick."

Charlie smiled devilishly. He didn't have to say anything else before she pounced on him like a lion on a hyena and straddled him. Their lips locked, and they kissed each other hungrily while yanking off their clothes.

They had made love so many times that right then, all Charlie wanted to do was fuck. Hard. When she threw her bra to the side, Mason's lips wrapped around the areola of one of her breasts. He flicked his tongue over her nipple, and she moaned at the beautiful sensation surging throughout her body. He knew she loved nipple play, and she quivered when she felt his fingers rolling her other nipple between them. Charlie let her head fall back, and she relished in the electrifying feeling of his mouth going back and forth between her breasts. He sucked and licked them until Charlie was wet and sticky between her thighs.

"Did I buy these?" Mason asked, tugging gently at her pink panties.

"Yes," she answered.

"I'll buy you some more," he said and ripped the panties off.

He pulled his thick dick out from the front of his boxers and pulled Charlie down on it. She cried out at the sudden pressure between her walls, and her pussy pulsated around his shaft. Wrapping her arms around his shoulders and looking him lustfully in the eye, Charlie prepared herself for a wild ride. Mason knew what it was she wanted, and he gave it to her relentlessly. He gripped her hips and began thrusting in and out of her wet and juicy cookie.

Charlie matched his thrusts because she wanted to fuck him back. She'd been missing her man, and she wanted to please him. She was sure the pleasured grimace on his face was the same one on hers.

When her legs got tired, he laid her on her back and spread her thighs. His eyes were on her fat pussy lips, and his thumb found her clit.

"Talking about is there somebody else when I got all this pussy right here," he said, rubbing her love button. "You think I would jeopardize myself like that and let another nigga get a chance at this pussy?"

"Mason . . ." Charlie moaned because he was rubbing an orgasm out of her.

"Cum for me. It's okay," he breathed. "Cum for me so I can stuff this big black dick back inside of you."

"Oh, Mason," Charlie cried, quivering. "I'm cumming. Oh my—oh my God. Mason!"

From her head to her toes, Charlie's body felt like an explosion went off inside of it. Her thick juices oozed out of her love tunnel, and Mason didn't give her time to catch her breath before he filled her up with his thick chocolate meat. He pressed his body on hers and commenced to pounding her out.

Charlie couldn't control her screams, and she hoped that she didn't wake MJ. Mason lasted about ten more minutes before Charlie could tell he couldn't take anymore.

"Hold on, baby. Don't cum yet," Charlie said. "Hit it like that a few more times. Yesss, like that. Like that, baby! Ohhh my Gooood! Yes!"

Mason's last thrust sent her into another climax. It was a good thing, too, because he wasn't able to hold back any longer. They came hard together in perfect harmony.

When they were done steadying their breathing, Mason picked Charlie up to take her to bed. As she placed her head on his chest, Charlie thought that maybe she hadn't lied to Mikayla. Maybe things were just fine between the two of them.

Or maybe she had thought too soon. The moment Charlie's head hit her pillow, Mason's phone started going off on the nightstand on his side of the bed.

"Hello?" He answered.

"Mason, it's almost eleven o'clock," Charlie whispered and made a face. "Come to bed."

Mason, still in nothing but his boxers, held up a finger to her. Charlie tried to make out the voice on the other end of the phone. She didn't know if she was making up things in her head or not, but she was almost certain that the voice belonged to a woman. Mason saw Charlie watching him, and not only did he turn away, but he stepped out into the hallway.

Charlie's curiosity had spiked, and when he came back in the room, she eyed him suspiciously. "Who was that?" she asked.

"Nobody," Mason said, avoiding eye contact.

"So why would they call you so late? And why did you have to go out there to take the call?"

"Charlie, it was nothing, all right?"

"Was it work?" Charlie asked, not letting up. "And if you don't answer me this time, you can take your pillow and go sleep on the wet spot on the couch tonight."

Mason sighed loudly, seeing that she really wasn't going to let it go. His hands went up but stopped at his waistline before he let them fall.

"It was work, okay? They want me to come in tonight, but I told them it's going to have to wait until the morning."

"You told them that?" Charlie asked, feeling the wolf in her calm down.

"Yes, I told them that," Mason said, turning off the light and climbing into bed with her. "Because all I want to do is sleep next to my beautiful lady and wake up and make my family a meal. Is that all right with you, woman?"

"That's all right with me," Charlie said and snuggled into his chest.

Chapter 3

Charlie

When Charlie opened her eyes, she was expecting to see Mason lying next to her, but his side of the bed was empty. She stretched before she sat up and glanced at the digital clock on her nightstand. The time read seven-thirty in the morning, and Charlie made a face. Mason didn't leave for work until nine. Where was he? She put her silk plum-colored robe on and left the bedroom.

She went downstairs, and from the kitchen, she heard someone bustling around like someone was in a hurry. She stood in the entrance of the kitchen and saw a figure standing by the fridge. It was dim, and the person's back was to her.

"Mason?" she called, but stayed at a distance just in case it wasn't him.

To her relief, Mason turned around. She flicked on the kitchen light and took notice that he was already dressed and had a lunch packed and ready to go.

"I'm sorry, baby. I didn't mean to wake you up before I left."

"You're heading into work a little early this morning. What, did someone die?" Charlie joked, but when she saw the look on his face, her eyes widened. "Someone died?"

"The landlord of an apartment complex thirty minutes from here kept getting complaints about a nasty smell coming from one of the units. He finally checked it out, and it turns out that there's a dead body inside. They want me to go to the crime scene to get ahead of the story."

"Okay, well, I'll get MJ off to daycare then."

"Daycare?" Mason asked and raised a brow. "I thought we agreed that MJ would stay home until he turns three."

"Yes, but with everything that I'm trying to do with my clothing line, I just need some extra time in my day. Time free of constantly making sure a two-year-old hasn't killed himself."

Mason gave Charlie a look, but he didn't say anything. He didn't have to. Charlie knew exactly what he was thinking. When he and Emerson were married, she had completely lost herself to her business. She had put Mason second to it, and Charlie knew how that had made him feel. But she was nothing like Emerson. She wasn't trying to start a business to run away from her feelings or problems. Charlie just wanted something for herself, something that she could pass down to her children. She had always been interested in clothing. In fact, when she was a teenager, she sometimes would make her own clothes.

Growing up, she didn't have much, so when she grew out of something, there wasn't money to get anything new. One day, she was so fed up with her ratty clothing she took two pairs of her old jeans and turned them into a jean jacket. When she returned to school the following day, all the kids were complimenting her new jacket and asking where she got it. It was then that she realized she had a talent, but life had made her forget her talent. It wasn't until she got with Mason and had the baby that she had even sat and thought about what else she wanted out of life.

She thought back to the day she decided to start her own business.

"I think I'm going to design my own clothes," Charlie had told Mason.

"That sounds great," he said.

"I'm going to make it into a business."

"I love the idea. Let me know what I can do to help."

"I will need some startup cash at first."

"Whatever you need."

That was the first and last time Mason seemed supportive of her dreams.

Charlie snapped out of her memory and continued her conversation with Mason.

"Mason, I—" She started, but his phone ringing interrupted her. He answered on the first ring.

"Hello?" he said into the receiver. "I'm walking out of the door now." He pulled the phone from his ear and put it to his chest. "I'm sorry, baby. We'll have to talk about this later. I gotta go."

He quickly kissed her on her lips and grabbed his lunch before he breezed past her. She didn't even get a chance to tell him that she loved him before he was gone. And just like that, she was alone again.

That was another reason Charlie wanted something of her own. She didn't anticipate the actual life of being the woman of a cop until she was in the position. She needed something to keep her mind busy from worry or any other thoughts that weren't positive. A business was the perfect thing. Not only would she have something to do, but she would carry a position that made her feel important every day.

She'd already begun designing her own dresses and bringing the prototypes to life. She named her clothing line Elegant by Charlie because all of her favorite designers had brands named after themselves. She knew there was nothing completely new under the sun, but still, she didn't want her gown line or store to be like any other. She wanted to specialize in event-wear and have something for all shapes and sizes. She could just see the beautiful gowns and dresses hanging in the window now. Everything was mapped out. The only thing missing was the startup money. She had thought about getting a loan, but Emerson had talked her into presenting her business plan to a few of her colleagues.

"Girl, don't go to no bank for a loan. It'll take forever, and they asking too many personal questions and pry into your life. And you know they add all these extra fees. Let me hook you up with my girl Shivelle. She is looking to invest. Her daddy left her enough money to buy a small island," Emerson said to Charlie.

"You really think so?"

"Yes. I've seen your business plan. It's tight. Shivelle is smart. She'll see you are a winning bet."

Charlie thought about it for a moment. She smiled. "Okay, hook a sista up."

Charlie and Emerson had met with Shivelle at the entrance to Cast Iron, the newest fine dining establishment in town.

"Shivelle, I'd like you to meet Charlie. Charlie, this is Shivelle."

Charlie shook Shivelle's hand. "It's a pleasure to meet you."

"The pleasure is all mine. Your business plan is very intriguing." Shivelle smiled.

They entered the restaurant. Charlie was stunned by the décor. It was simple and elegant. The high ceilings with the crystal chandeliers made the space feel even bigger than it was. The muted colors brought a warmth to the space. The layout was such that you felt a part of the dining room and the other patrons, but separate enough that you could have a conversation without worrying everyone would be listening in.

"This place is stunning," Charlie commented.

"If your business is as successful as I predict, you'll be dining at restaurants like this all the time," Shivelle said then greeted the maître d'.

Shivelle ordered a bottle of wine as soon as they sat down. When they each had a glass, Shivelle raised hers to make a toast. "To a successful partnership." They all tapped their wine glasses together and took a sip.

Charlie couldn't believe her dream was about to be reality. "So, what happens now?"

"I'll have my attorney draw up our agreement, and once those get signed, we make Elegant by Charlie the massive success it should be. With your creativity and my business acumen, I envision opening two more stores in a year."

"Are you serious?" Charlie was stunned.

"Absolutely. It depends on how your first store does the first year, but I'm predicting big numbers the first year."

Charlie was ready to get to work immediately. She wanted to jump up and scream in celebration, but she held it together. Instead, she just squeezed Emerson's knee under the table. Emerson looked at Charlie with a big smile on her face.

The rest of the lunch was more of a get-to-know-you session. Shivelle and Charlie hit it off, and Charlie felt confident that she was in good hands with Shivelle.

Three weeks later, with all the paperwork signed, Charlie was scheduled to see a space for her store.

After Charlie dropped MJ off at daycare at around noon, she ventured off to meet a real estate agent. Her name was Shirley Prichard, and Shivelle had asked her to show Charlie a spot she thought would be perfect for Elegant by Charlie. The place was in downtown Baltimore, and Charlie knew she was going to just love it. It was downtown, after all. The location itself would bring in traffic.

When she reached the destination, Charlie parked her 2019 Toyota Camry on the curb behind a gold Ford Explorer. Standing in front of an empty storefront was a skinny, blond-haired woman in a pantsuit. She was smiling as Charlie made her way toward her, and she held out her hand.

"Charlie, I presume?"

"You are correct," Charlie answered and shook her hand with a warm smile of her own. She then looked behind her at the place she was going to show. It wasn't attached to any other business and had its own parking lot. Through the window, Charlie could tell that it was a nice-sized space.

"Perfect. I'm Shirley, and I'll be showing you this beautiful property."

"Sounds good to me. Lead the way," Charlie told her.

"You're going to *love* this space," Shirley said, pulling a set of keys from her pocket. "They usually say to save the best for last, but I'm making an exception this time. That's not to say that the other places aren't as nice. This one just personally gives me that *wow factor*. Come on."

She unlocked the glass front door with one of her keys and opened the door wide enough for Charlie to get through. *Wow factor* was right. Even the air inside smelled great. It fit her vision perfectly for Elegant, all the way down to the placement of the dressing rooms.

"It was a boutique prior to being placed on the market," Shirley said, noticing Charlie's gaze. "Feel free to move around as you wish. There are two bathroom facilities as well."

Charlie did as Shirley suggested and looked around. The only thing in the whole place that Charlie didn't like was that the floors were carpeted. "Can I pull this carpet up and put in hardwood floors?"

"I'd have to ask the landlord. Maybe he would do it for you."

"What made the owner want to sell?" Charlie asked curiously.

"They actually opened up another store at a bigger location."

"Bigger than this?" Charlie asked and looked around.

"Yes, so there is no question whether you would have traffic with Elegant. This location is just marvelous for shopping, so that's definitely a plus."

"If I'm being all the way honest, everything here is a plus," Charlie said with a smile. "I can already see my evening gowns in the window there. And my bridal area can be set up over there and, oh my goodness, this place is even big enough if I decide to carry intimates! I love it!"

"I knew you would," Shirley told her. "And you'll also be pleased to know that the previous owners took *very* good care of the property. They renovated the entire building and redid the electrical wiring last year."

"So, in other words, I would be able to open up whenever."

"Whenever we close a deal," Shirley said in a slightly suggestive way.

Charlie looked around the place one last time. She could have sworn it started to sparkle like a diamond. She couldn't believe how perfect it was. Could it be too good to be true?

No, Charlie. No negative thoughts, she told herself. *There is no such thing as too good to be true when you work hard.*

"Okay, let's do it," Charlie said out loud. "I'll contact Shivelle so that we can put in an offer."

"Great," Shirley said and shook Charlie's hand again. "I look forward to hearing from you guys."

Charlie thanked her and left. She still had some hours before she had to go get MJ from daycare, so she thought maybe she could grab some lunch with Mason.

Once she was seated comfortably in her car, she pulled her cell phone from her purse and called him.

"I was just about to call you," Mason said as soon as he picked up.

"Great minds," Charlie said, smiling to herself. "Were you wanting to go grab some lunch too?"

"I'm afraid that my call to you wasn't going to be so pleasant," he said in a strained voice. "Do you know where Mikayla is?"

"Umm, it's a little after one on a Saturday. She's probably at home with the girls."

"You might want to get over to her house and fast. Something happened."

"Something happened? Something like what happened?"

"Something terrible."

Chapter 4

Emerson

Emerson felt herself doing it again. And by "it," she meant she felt herself pulling away. She sat at a glass table wrapped in a satin robe across from the man who was falling in love with her. Jacob Andrews had admitted to her the night before that he was indeed falling for her, and afterward, they had fantastic sex. But now, there Emerson was, dealing with the real after effects of him declaring something so serious to her. She was still figuring out how she felt about him, but up until that moment, he was winning. Now she felt rushed, even though he told her not to feel that way.

Emerson wanted to take things slow. It had been a while since she was with someone who she clicked so much with. She had been enjoying her time with Jacob, but now there was nothing she wanted to do more than make a beeline for the door. But she didn't, because that would be rude. Also, he'd made brunch, and Emerson was hungry. Still, she didn't know what to say, so instead, she sipped her orange juice and ate her food.

"You okay, baby?" Jacob asked from the other side of the table. "You've barely said a thing all morning."

She hadn't realized until then that he'd been watching her. He had a curious look in his eyes as he chewed his bacon. Emerson felt the conversation she didn't want to have sizzling up.

"I'm just a little tired. You wore me out last night," she said, throwing his ego a bone.

It worked, because Jacob started cheesing like a Cheshire cat. "I tore that thang up, didn't I?" he asked jokingly.

"You are a mess," she told him. "What do you have planned for the rest of the day?"

"I was hoping that you and I could spend some more time together," he hinted, and Emerson almost choked on her juice.

"Oh, honey, I'm sorry," Emerson said, thinking quick. "I have that dinner tonight."

"Dinner?"

"Yeah, remember the one I told you about? With the owner of that makeup company?"

"Nooo . . ." Jacob said, really trying to wrack his memory. "I'm sorry I don't, babe. But I'll get better at remembering those kinds of things. If it's important to you, it's important to me."

Emerson felt a rush of emotion overcome her. It had only been seven months, but Jacob had really impressed her. He was fine as hell, with smooth peanut-butter skin and a low-cut fade. His mustache was always neatly trimmed, and his jawline was something to be envious of. Jacob was a lawyer at a firm, and that was actually how Emerson had met him.

"Where the hell is he at?" Emerson said out loud.

She was standing outside of a courtroom, waiting impatiently for her legal council to show up. Court was set to start in five minutes, and Eddie, her lawyer, was nowhere to be found. Emerson had called his phone a few times, but it rang all the way through to voicemail. She was beginning to panic, because the last thing she wanted to do was continue the case out, especially since it was for something as small as a fender bender.

She hadn't been paying attention one day, backing out of a parking spot, and bumped into someone. Jamie Letters was her name, and the moment she found out she'd been hit by Emerson Dayle, she'd been trying to sue her for a fortune. Emerson couldn't believe the woman was acting like that. She barely had any damage to her car. Jamie claimed that she'd hit her head and gotten whiplash, and also that her back had been in pain ever since. It was ridiculous, and Emerson was just ready for it to be over so that she could go back to work.

"Emerson? Emerson Dayle?"

Emerson whipped around toward the voice calling her name and saw that it belonged to a handsome black man wearing a two-button suit. She had never seen him a day in her life, so she had no idea how he knew her name. He approached her holding a black briefcase and extended his hand.

"My name is Jacob Andrews. I work at the same firm as Eddie."

"Well, where the hell is Eddie?" Emerson asked tersely. "Court is about to start."

"Eddie isn't going to make it," Jacob said and instantly started talking faster after seeing the look overcome Emerson. "Something very serious came up, but that's why I'm here, and I want to assure you that you can put your complete confidence in me. I also will probably do a better job than my colleague."

Emerson didn't laugh at his joke. She didn't even crack a smile. Instead, she stood there and tried to calm herself down. She was still taking her medication, just not as heavy a dose. She was learning to cope with things in better ways, and one of them was not letting things that upset her control her. She wanted nothing more than to scream and turn the entire courthouse upside down, but she couldn't do that. The goal was to get back to work, not to get behind bars.

"This can't be happening." She groaned out loud.

"Well, it is, and, oh, here, I brought these for you," Jacob said, reaching into his briefcase and pulling out a handful of caramel candies. "I read a few things from your file."

"My love for caramel isn't in any file," Emerson said, looking curiously at him.

"This is true. I actually found out about your love for caramel candies through your social media. In your file, I found out that—"

"I'm a crazy bitch," she finished for him.

"That sometimes things upset you," he finished for himself. "So, I took the liberty of trying to find something that might keep you calm."

"And you did all of that this morning?"

"I'm a black lawyer, which means I'm always in the white man's playground. I've learned to be quick and diligent about anything I want to know. This time, it happened to be you."

"Hmm," Emerson said, trying to ignore the peculiar look in his eye.

"Lets get in there before the judge. After you," Jacob said and pushed the door to the courtroom open.

Jamie saw Emerson enter and had a smug look on her face. She was suing Emerson for fifty thousand dollars and was apparently expecting to get every cent of it. Her lawyer held a look of confidence on his face as well. It took every inch of self-control she had to not roll her eyes in their direction. Instead, she followed Jacob to the front of the courtroom and stood beside him.

"What do I say?" Emerson leaned and whispered to Jacob.

Eddie had prepped her over the phone, but all of his council had gone out the window. Emerson had no reason to trust the advice of a man that she couldn't even trust to show up to court. She made a mental note to get her retainer fee back.

"You don't have to do anything but sit there and look pretty," he told her and flashed his pearly whites at her.

She didn't know whether to be confident or afraid of his confidence.

Judge Marren entered the courtroom and everyone rose. The judge sat and said, "Please be seated."

The judge first asked Jamie why she was suing Emerson.

"The defendant reversed her vehicle into my client's car, Your Honor," Jamie's lawyer answered. "She suffered a head and back injury."

"Do you have any documents showing these facts?" Judge Marren asked.

"Yes. Here are my client's hospital documents from after the accident. Also, she has been going to a chiropractor for her back pain. She is suing for medical reimbursement, damage to her vehicle, and emotional support."

The judge motioned for the documents to be brought to him, and while he looked over the papers, Emerson felt herself growing fidgety. She didn't know Jamie had done all of that while waiting for the court date. What a deceiving little—

"Counselor Andrews, are you and your client making a dispute today?"

"Yes," Jacob said. "The grocery store's surveillance footage from that day disappeared, but luckily someone accidentally recorded the whole thing on their phone. I have a video from Shantell Wright, who was innocently recording her daughter helping with groceries when the

accident took place in the background. If you watch the video, you can clearly see that yes, my client reversed her car into the other. However, the impact was barely enough to rock a sleeping baby awake. I do believe that when Miss Jamie Letters learned that the person who hit her car was my client, she saw this as an opportunity to make a quick buck."

"How are you going to tell me what I felt when she hit my car? I hit my head!" Jamie said, glaring at Jacob.

"Not hard enough to forget about a quick comeup," Jacob said and pulled something from his briefcase. "I have here a sworn statement obtained by my colleague from a former employee from that grocery store who says Jamie paid him four hundred dollars to erase the camera footage from that day—with the promise that another payment would be paid out when she got the money from suing Emerson Dayle."

Jamie's lawyer looked from the paper in Jacob's hand to Jamie with a sour look on his face. He hadn't been expecting that, and truth be told, neither was Emerson. The sinking feeling she'd had in her stomach went away, and she felt relief come over her when Jamie didn't try to fight Jacob's words.

"Is what he's saying true, Miss Letters?" the judge asked. "Remember, you are under oath."

"I–I. Oh. Okay, so what. None of that takes away from the fact that she hit me! What's fifty grand to her anyways? I mean, look at her. That's a Chanel bag, for crying out loud."

"Your Honor, I move for this case to be tossed out. Mrs. Dayle's insurance has already fixed the damage on Miss Letters' car, and I think at this point, she should hope that my client doesn't seek justice for the false accusations."

"Miss Letters, making false statements as you have is a criminal offense punishable by jail time," Judge Marren said and banged his gavel.

"Jail?" Jamie's eyes bulged out of her head.

"No," Emerson spoke up. "I don't want to press charges."

"All right, then. Well, from the evidence gathered here today, I am going to grant the motion to toss this case out. Court is adjourned."

The judge banged the gavel down, and there was a wide smile on Emerson's face. She was happy that she hadn't had to show her ass and ruin her Chanel pantsuit. Turning to Jacob, she shook his hand.

"Thank you," she said. "I appreciate you for showing up today. I was thinking about asking Eddie for my retainer back, but now I'm just going to give it to you."

"I'll be sure to tell Eddie to give me my money when I get back to the office today." Jacob chuckled.

"Oh, and its Ms. Dayle. You called me Mrs., and I'm divorced. I just haven't changed my last name back yet."

"Oh, I apologize. I guess I didn't research as well as I thought."

"It's okay," Emerson said with a smile. "You know what? How about you let me buy you lunch? If you don't have to go right back to the office."

"No, I can't let you do that. That wouldn't be appropriate."

"I'm sorry," Emerson said quickly. "I didn't mean to offend you."

"Well, you did. A beautiful woman like yourself should never take a man out to eat. Even as a reward. Queens get treated, and whereas I actually do need to get back to the office, I would love to treat you to dinner this evening."

"Oh, wow." She had to catch her breath. She hadn't expected him to say all of that. "Okay. What time?"

"Does seven work for you?"

"I'll make it work."

"Perfect. I have your number. I'll give you a call around then."

"Okay. It's a date."

At the time, Emerson had no idea that Jacob would become a constant part of her life for the months to come. The thing that she liked most about Jacob was that he accepted her. She didn't have to hide who she was when she was feeling any emotion. She was able to be herself with him, and he didn't treat her any differently. That scared her. In fact, it terrified her to *see* someone care about her so effortlessly.

She felt like trash for lying to him, and it felt like all the walls were closing in on her. She needed some air.

"Excuse me," she said and pushed back from the table.

She hurried to his bedroom before he could say anything to stop her. Once there, she plopped down on his bed and breathed deeply. Getting closer to Jacob was starting to make Emerson feel like she wasn't in control. She was feeling things she hadn't felt in years, so she didn't know how to handle them. All the techniques she'd learned in counseling to get a hold of her emotions weren't working. The only thing she could do was breathe and count her breaths to steady the thumping in her chest.

She heard the faint sound of something vibrating, and when she looked in the direction of where it was coming from, she saw her Celine bag. She knew her phone was at the bottom of it, so she went over, reached in, and grabbed it.

Charlie's contact photo was on the screen. It had taken a while, but she was glad that the two of them were friends again. Words couldn't describe how much Emerson loved her nephew and what having him in her life meant to her.

"Hey, Charlie," Emerson answered, and when she listened to the other end, she heard panting. "Are you okay?"

"Eme, I need you to get down here right now! Mikayla's mother was just found murdered."

Chapter 5

Mikayla

Mikayla stood as still as a gargoyle as she looked down at her mother's motionless face. Her eyes were closed, and her hair was disheveled. She actually looked like she often did when Mikayla was younger and Jewel was passed out, high. Except this time, Jewel wouldn't be waking up.

The morgue was cold, both literally and figuratively. The gray concrete walls and fluorescent lighting made it an uninviting space. One wall was covered in small metal doors, behind each one a dead body waiting to be identified or autopsied.

Mikayla's eyes went to the deep gashes on Jewel's face and the bruises on her cheeks. By the way her mouth was positioned, it looked like her jaw had been broken. Anybody else might have shed a few tears seeing their mother like that, but not Mikayla. She knew the shady life Jewel lived and also knew that there were only a few ways a life like that could end.

Mikayla's jaw tensed, and she peered at Jewel for a few more moments before stepping back from the table. She nodded her head at the detective standing next to her.

"That's her," she said, identifying the body.

She felt the warm touches of Emerson and Charlie on her shoulders. They'd come as her comfort and moral support. Mikayla cleared her throat and focused her attention on Detective Janes.

"That's my mother."

"Thank you for your cooperation, Mrs. King. I'll have someone follow up with you."

"Do you—does anyone know what happened?" she asked.

"Torture," Detective Janes told her. "And from the looks of the crime scene, it had to have been terrible. To keep her quiet, she had to have been gagged, and there would have had to be a lot of background noise."

"Torture? Why would someone torture her?"

"We think that your mother may have had something the perpetrator wanted. Do you know anything about that?"

"No. She didn't have anything," Mikayla said. "She never had anything."

"That doesn't look like the case, unfortunately," he said. "I'm going to do everything in my power to find out who did this to her. In the meantime, I'll leave you to start sorting out funeral arrangements."

"Funeral arrangements?" Mikayla asked, slightly alarmed.

"Yes, if you are her next of kin, then the decision lies with you. Burial or cremation."

"Well, you can burn the bitch for all I care!"

"Mikayla!" Charlie exclaimed from behind her.

"I'll be in touch. Excuse me," the detective said, clearly wanting no parts in that conversation.

"That woman did nothing for me my entire life," Mikayla said when he was gone. "And when she finally does get the chance to be in it and *maybe* form a relationship, what does she do? Show up on my doorstep with my brother and—"

She stopped speaking abruptly, realizing she almost said too much. Instead, she saved herself with a frustrated sigh and squeezed her fists together.

"She's still your mother," Charlie told her.

"And for that, I will pay for her cremation. But I will *not* pay for or have a funeral for a woman so evil. Damian can have her ashes."

Charlie and Emerson exchanged a look but didn't say anything. Ever since Mikayla and Charlie had been separated, she had been more unapologetically vocal. She wanted to tell them that she honestly didn't care about their opinions on the topic because neither had been in her shoes. Jewel had never loved Mikayla, and if Damian were smart, he would see that she didn't love him either. He blamed Mikayla for the situation he was in when in truth, it was Jewel. She was a terrible mother when he was free, but when he was locked up, she was able to get in his head. In a sense, Mikayla was happy that she wouldn't have to worry about Jewel popping up and bribing her for more money. She didn't feel that Damian was smart enough to do something like that on his own. Still, now that Jewel was dead, she knew she would have to have some sort of contact with her brother.

"Lets go," she said to her friends. "It smells like death in here."

"Well, we are in a freaking morgue," Emerson said and pinched her nose. "Yeah, let's get out of here. My skin is crawling."

"What, are you afraid one of the bodies will start trying to get out?" Charlie teased.

"I'm not staying to find out!" Emerson said. She was the first one on her way to the door.

Mikayla looked back one last time as the coroner was placing a blanket over her mother's face. Death was sad, but a painful death was something to make a heart wretch. No tears came down, but still she felt a small longing. She wondered what it would have been like to grow up in a normal household, not with a drug-addicted mother.

She'd never told Charlie or Emerson that she'd seen her mother again when she was eighteen. It was a memory that she'd tried to wipe.

"Mine!" Mikayla spun in a circle in the living room of her new one-bedroom apartment.

It wasn't much, but it was hers. The only furniture she had was the bedroom set in her room, but she knew the rest would come. She had turned eighteen recently and was released from foster care. She had been preparing for that day for some years, working and saving her money since she was fifteen years old. She didn't want to end up on the streets just because someone wasn't getting a check for her anymore. She used her savings to get a place and a car to get her back and forth from work.

Mikayla was beyond excited. The movers had just finished putting up her bedroom set and had left, so it was her first time really alone in the place. She stared at the two golden keys in her hand and thought that life was looking up. The place was nice. Stainless steel appliances and nice-sized rooms. It wasn't the big house that she always wanted, but it was a good start. She couldn't wait to invite Eme and Charlie over for a girl's night.

Just as she was about to go lay down on her bed and watch some television before she had to go to work, she heard her phone ringing. Pulling it from her back pocket, she glanced at the screen and saw a number she didn't know. Mikayla contemplated ignoring the call, but flipped it open out of curiosity.

"Hello?"

"Kay Kay?"

Mikayla felt all the blood in her face drain, and air got caught in her throat. She hadn't heard the voice in years, but she would recognize it anywhere. The hairs on the back of her neck stood up as she regained her wits.

"Jewel," Mikayla said, calling her mother by her first name. "How did you get this number?"

"Your old high school gave it to me when I called there," Jewel answered.

"Well, what do you want?"

"What? No 'Hi, Mom. How are you?' You get right to the point, don't you?"

"You can either tell me what you want or get hung up on. The choice is yours," Mikayla said, hearing the distaste dripping from her tongue.

"Okay, okay, okay," Jewel sighed. "I know things between us haven't been good, but that shit is in the past. You're eighteen now and grown. The thing is, I need you, Kay Kay. If you can just come to where I'm at."

"I have to work in a few hours."

"This won't take but thirty minutes. I just want to see you."

Mikayla was quiet. She hadn't seen or spoken to Jewel in years. Jewel put up a front like she was upset that her kids were in the system, yet never straightened up to get them out. Mikayla didn't know what she wanted to do. She didn't know what she would do when she saw her mother. Would she hug her or smack the shit out of her? She wouldn't know unless she went.

"All right. Are you at home? Or somewhere else?"

"At home. I have a new address. I'll text it to you."

"Okay. I'm on my way once I receive it."

"Good. I can't wait to see you," Jewel said, sounding happy.

When they got off the phone, Mikayla found herself wondering if Jewel had finally gotten sober. Mikayla hoped that was the case. She had to see her.

When the text message with the address came through, Mikayla left her cozy new dwelling to head over there. The place was about twenty minutes away from Mikayla's apartment. It was a small house with a gate around it, a Chevy Impala parked in the driveway, and neatly trimmed grass. Mikayla opened the door to the gate and walked up to the door. The house was in good shape, which made Mikayla hopeful that her mother was now sober and being responsible.

She knocked on the door. It opened seconds later, and standing before her was a smiling Jewel. Mikayla took in her image and had to admit that she looked healthier. She was never an ugly woman, but now she looked more well groomed. She had a new wig on her head and wore a cute romper outfit. She even had on some mascara and lip gloss.

"Kay Kay!" She squealed and hugged her daughter. "You don't understand how happy I am that you came. Don't just stand there. Come in!"

Mikayla hesitated but ultimately entered the home. It smelled like vanilla. Looking around, she couldn't even say something like "This is definitely my mom's house," because she never knew what Jewel liked. Their old house didn't have any décor—just a couch, a TV, and mattresses on the floor of the bedrooms.

Something didn't feel right. Mikayla felt like she was in a staged house that a realtor was preparing to show. Everything inside was neat and tidy, and it looked like Jewel had come into some money somewhere.

"You hungry?"

"No."

"Thirsty?"

"No."

"Well, I'm going to get you a glass of water anyway," Jewel told her and pointed to the living room. "Go and

have a seat. I opened the blinds for you because it just looks so nice in here when the natural light hits."

"Natural light?" Mikayla mumbled to herself.

She'd never heard her mother speak like that, and it was throwing her off. She was used to the mean and bitter woman that was always looking for money for the next hit. The couch she sat on was comfortable but firm underneath her. The living room had a silver and glass color scheme going on, and the turquoise-colored couches went well.

Jewel joined her and sat next to her on the couch.

"Here you go," Jewel said and handed Mikayla a glass of water.

"Thanks, I guess," Mikayla said, looking around some more. "You look like you've been doing well for yourself."

"I just wanted something more for myself." Jewel shrugged. "I didn't want to stay in our old dump forever."

"You working now?"

"Yeah. I work at a call center."

"Hmm." Mikayla nodded and took a sip from her glass. "You clean?"

"I smoke weed all day, but I don't touch anything else."

"Good for you. So, what is it that you wanted me to come over here for? It looks like you've been living a good life. One that's fine without me in it."

"I just—I wanted to make things right between us," Jewel said, and Mikayla tried to find the sincerity in her eyes. "And . . . and talk to you about your brother."

There it was.

"I've been putting money on his books since I was fifteen. More than enough."

"He's been trying to call you. He says you don't answer the phone."

"I'm always at work when he calls, and it's not like I can call back," Mikayla said bluntly. "Have you put any money on his books?"

"When I'm able," Jewel said, and Mikayla knew that meant no.

"It looks like you're more than able. You weren't a mother to us when you had us, but you can at least be one to Damian now."

"I didn't call you over here to argue," Jewel said, and Mikayla saw a familiar flicker in her eye. It was the same flicker she'd seen growing up, the one that let her know that her mother was losing her patience.

"Then what else do you want to talk about?"

The words hadn't left her mouth when she heard the front door open and close. Jewel didn't budge or look shocked that someone had come inside her home. She must have been expecting them. Mikayla gave her a skeptical look and swiveled her head to see who had just come in the house. A tall, chocolate man wearing a suit walked toward them.

"The front door was unlocked," he said, speaking to Jewel but keeping his eyes on Mikayla.

"I'm sorry, baby. My daughter just got here. I must have forgotten to lock it back," Jewel said quickly. "Mikayla, this is my old man, Donnie. Donnie, this is Mikayla."

"I've heard so much about you," Donnie said as his eyes ran over Mikayla's whole body. "Beautiful just like your mama. I can't wait to get to know you better. All of you."

"Go on back to the room, baby. It won't be much longer."

Donnie licked his lips at both of them and made his exit. Mikayla didn't like how he had been looking at her. There was something about the hungry look in his eyes that made her skin crawl. She was ready to leave.

"That is actually something else I wanted to talk to you about," Jewel stated.

"About your boyfriend? Is he beating your ass or something?"

Jewel gave Mikayla a knowing look. *"You're older now, and one day you'll understand that things between a man and his woman aren't always black and white,"* she said, clearing her throat. *"Donnie is a businessman, and he's good to me. Except sometimes . . ."*

"Sometimes what?"

"He gets a little upset when things don't go his way. He might get physical, or he might leave, and I can't afford this house by myself."

"So what does any of that have to do with me?"

Jewel grabbed hold of Mikayla's hands. *"A little while back, I came across your photo in the newspaper. You had done something noteworthy at school, and you were so cute with your hair down and your dress on. Well, Donnie saw the picture, and he asked when you turned eighteen. I told him, and . . . and . . ."*

"And what?" Mikayla asked, feeling all the moisture drying up in her mouth.

"He wants you, Kay Kay," Jewel told Mikayla, looking into her daughter's growing eyes. *"Just for one night. And I won't even be mad about it. I just need to make sure my bills get paid and Donnie doesn't leave me."*

Mikayla was shocked. She was frozen, numb, and couldn't even feel Jewel's hands on hers. She couldn't believe what she was hearing. It had been years since she'd even seen Jewel, and when she did, she was trying to pimp her out. The rage was boiling behind her sadness, but both feelings were coming full force.

"You're willing to sell me, your own flesh and blood, to a man?" Mikayla whispered, feeling the tears coming to her eyes. *"You want me to fuck him?"*

"Baby, please. Just do it for me. He's a gentle lover. He won't hurt you, Kay Kay."

"Don't call me that!" Mikayla said and snatched her hands away. "I didn't even want to come here, but something in me said that you might really be trying to right your wrongs. I should've listened to my gut instinct. Fuck you! Never call me again."

Mikayla tried to get up and head for the door, but Jewel pulled her back down on the couch.

"You ungrateful little bitch. You owe me!" Jewel sneered, getting close to Mikayla's face. "You ruined my life, having those white folks all up in my business and getting my money cut off! It was hard for me, and now that I finally have something nice, you're going to help me!"

"I'm not helping with anything," Mikayla shouted back. "You were a terrible mother! I had to get us out of there."

"And you see how that worked out, huh? Your brother is in jail!"

"And that would have never happened if you took care of the kids you popped out. Junkie bitch." Mikayla stood up and spit on the carpet by Jewel's feet. "You ain't never gon' be shit, and your life is almost half over. That's a shame. I never want to see you again." Mikayla jerked away from Jewel and stormed out of the house.

Mikayla came back to reality and blinked her eyes a few times. The coroner was putting Jewel back on ice, and Mikayla wanted to catch up to her friends. She was sad about the torture Jewel suffered, but she had lived a dirty life, and it had finally caught up to her.

Chapter 6

Emerson

If Mikayla had been anyone else, Emerson would have never been that close to a dead body. But she wanted to support her friend. Afterward, the women went to get a drink because after that, nobody really had an appetite.

They sat in a bar called Mosey's, a place that Emerson had suggested. She'd done her own Taste of Baltimore in the summer, where she ate at different restaurants and bars around the city and rated them to her following. Any participating restaurant had to pay her a fee, of course, and Mosey's was one of those places. It was in her top five, and she figured it would be perfect for the occasion. It was a chill environment, and right then, she was sure no one needed anything over the top.

"I wonder what the fuck happened to her," Charlie said out loud.

"Charlie!" Emerson exclaimed, almost choking on her martini.

"You saw her face, Eme. Her jaw was broken. And those cuts? Did you see how deep they were? I've only seen shit like that in movies. Mikayla, was your mom involved in anything crazy?"

"When *wasn't* she involved in something crazy?" Mikayla said, shaking her head. "Her entire life was a whirlpool of crazy. There's no telling what could have happened to her. Hopefully, the detective will find out

and let us know something. In the meantime, I can't
believe I'm stuck with the bill for her funeral."

"Have you talked to Damian?"

"Not in a while, but I'll have to soon. I'm sure he'll be
popping up around here," Mikayla said and then shook
her head. "You know, I didn't even know she was back in
Baltimore. Shit, I didn't know where she was."

Emerson watched as an uneasy look came over
Mikayla's face, but it was only there for a moment. By
the time Emerson blinked and looked again, it was gone.
She didn't know what was going on in her friend's mind,
but she knew it couldn't be good. Before Charlie could
open her mouth to continue that conversation, Emerson
butted in.

"Well, like you said, it's in the detective's hands now.
How's everything going with The Sisterhood? Don't you
have a luncheon coming up?"

"Everything is going good," Mikayla answered, looking
genuinely relieved to have a change in conversation. "Yes,
we do have our Empowering with Love Luncheon coming
up in a few weeks. Are you guys going to be able to make
it?"

"Wouldn't miss it," Charlie said and waved the bartender down. When the young girl came over, Charlie
pointed at her empty glass. "Can I have another Long
Island?"

"Of course. I'll be right back," the bartender said and
took the glass from her. "Anybody else need anything?"

"No, we're good," Emerson said, still working on her
first Long Island. When the bartender was gone, she
turned her attention back to Mikayla. "Of course I'm
going to be there. Seeing you blossom into this bad-ass
super bitch is amazing."

"And will you be coming alone, Eme, or will there be a
plus one?" Charlie asked, her voice implying that she was
insinuating something.

"And what exactly is that supposed to mean?"

Charlie shrugged. "All I'm saying is that you're glowing, and your ass has been sitting up like somebody is hitting it on the regular."

Emerson cut her eyes at Mikayla, who shook her finger.

"Unh-uh, don't look at me like that. I didn't say anything," Mikayla said.

"She didn't. I guessed," Charlie said truthfully. "And I can't believe that you wouldn't tell me that you have a new man!"

"First of all, let me stop you there. He's not my man," Emerson told her. "We just enjoy each other's company."

"How long have you guys been dating?"

"Seven months."

"Seven months!" Charlie exclaimed. "You've just been enjoying each other's company for seven months?"

"Yes. What's wrong with that?" Emerson asked, and both Charlie and Mikayla exchanged a look. "What?"

"So, it's not anything serious?"

"I mean . . ." Emerson's voice trailed off as she remembered what Jacob had told her the night before. "I guess you can say that. He told me he's falling in love with me, but I'm just not ready for any kind of label, and I don't know how to tell Jacob that."

"Jacob? You don't really look like the type to date a Jacob," Charlie said.

"Charlie!" That time it was Mikayla yelling her name.

By then, the bartender had returned with Charlie's drink, and she was kept preoccupied for a moment.

Mikayla turned back to Emerson and pursed her lips.

"What?" Emerson asked.

"So, this man told you he's falling in love with you, and all you're worried about is labels? Well, what did you say back?"

"I didn't say anything. I just fucked his brains out. And this morning, I felt like I couldn't breathe."

"So, this is super recent, as in last night recent." Mikayla's eyes widened. "Oh, wow, Eme. What are you going to do?"

"I just like things the way they are, you know? Why do we have to rush into something more serious?"

"You think seven months is rushing?"

"To me it is. I don't want to jump into a relationship with this man just because he thinks he's falling in love with me. Don't my feelings count?"

"Well, how do you feel, Eme?" Charlie asked, rejoining the conversation.

"I . . . I feel like I like him a lot. He's so good to me, and he makes me happy. It's just . . ."

"It's just what?"

"Yeah, we're your girls. You can tell us anything," Mikayla encouraged her.

"I'm just getting to the point where I can control my emotional reactions to certain things. I've been doing a lot of natural remedies, and my psychiatrist has even been lowering the dosage of my medication because I've made so much progress. But—" Emerson sighed. "I'm worried that a relationship might trigger emotions I haven't mastered yet. I don't want to spiral out of control ever again. After that whole debacle with Mason, I never want to feel that lonely again. I don't want to lose myself."

Emerson blinked a few tears away. Charlie had a shocked and guilty look on her face.

"Don't worry, Charlie. I don't blame you for anything. I'm happy that you and Mason are in love." It felt good to be able to talk so openly and freely about her issues to her friends. That was something she had never done before. She'd gotten so accustomed to acting like nothing was wrong that she'd never felt the need to discuss anything.

Now she understood the key to true happiness was being true to who you are, and that meant unlocking every locked door inside of her and facing each problem head on.

"I understand where you're coming from. I really do," Mikayla said. "But if this man has been this patient with you and makes you feel how you've been looking lately, don't you think it's worth a shot? I mean, if love ever comes around again for me, I might be a little apprehensive too . . . but I'm never going to stop giving up on my happily ever after."

"I'll think about it," Emerson told her. "But that's the best I can do right now."

"And I'll take that." Mikayla smiled. "Charlie, what's been going on with Elegant?"

The question made Charlie's face light up, and Emerson knew she must have some good news.

"You guys, everything is coming together so seamlessly. I feel like I'm starring in one of those rags to riches Lifetime movies. I never thought I would have any of what I have now, so seeing even more manifest in front of me brings me so much joy," she said, beaming. "Shivelle had me look at a place earlier today downtown that would be the perfect location. I *loved* it. I shot her an email while we were on the way here, and she made an offer!"

"Oh my God!" Emerson clapped her hands. "That is fantastic, Charlie!"

"Thank you. When I say this place is perfect, it's *perfect*. I couldn't have done it without you, Eme. I love you forever."

"I just placed a few dots. You did the connecting all on your own. When do you project to be open for business?"

"Even though we will have the store's location, I still don't want to rush it. I want to do a few runway shows here and a few other cities to get some buzz going about my designs. Shivelle has already set me up with a few well known people who have requested customized gowns for events. So, hopefully not only will that put a nice chunk of change in my pocket, but it will help with the growth of Elegant as a serious and upscale clothing company."

"And how is Mason taking to this new business adventure of yours?" Emerson asked. She knew how he had been with her when she was growing a business. He acted like a little kid who needed attention every second he thought he should have it. It made it difficult to be an individual. When they were married, he'd wanted her to fit his puzzle, not have her own. It might not have been so bad if he was trying to fit her puzzle too, but he wasn't. He had been so self-interested that it made her the same way. She hated that what was important to her wasn't important to him, yet he'd expected her to be excited about everything he wanted in life. By the looks of it, things hadn't changed, and Emerson was shocked. She thought that he would have learned from his mistake.

Charlie shook her head. "I don't know. It's like he just doesn't even think to care," she said. "He loves me. I know he does. But when it comes to this business venture, he could be a little more supportive. He wanted me to stay home with MJ until he was three, but I just can't do that."

"Doesn't he know who you have investing in you?" Emerson asked, wrinkling her forehead.

"No, I haven't told him," Charlie said. "I honestly haven't seen much of Mason lately. Between his crazy schedule at work and the fact that even when he's home we don't spend time together, I don't know what's going on with us. Aht!" Charlie raised her hand at Mikayla, who had just opened her mouth to talk. "I know I didn't tell the complete truth last night at your house. I just didn't want to put another weight on your shoulders."

"Talking about real things happening in your life is never a weight, Charlie," Mikayla said. "And I think you should tell Mason. Maybe if he knew Shivelle Stine was the one investing in you, he would be right there by your side."

"I want his support to be genuine, not because a big name is beside mine."

"Sometimes people need a real fact like that to know that you're serious," Emerson said. "Don't pull away from him. Include him. Let him see firsthand how important this clothing line is to you. You already gave him the one thing he wanted in this world. Now it's time to give someone else the same thing."

"I heard that." Mikayla raised her glass. "Now, if only Charles would take that advice and sign the damn divorce papers!"

The girls shared a laugh, but Emerson's heart really went out to Mikayla. Not only had Charles done a number on her mentally, emotionally, and physically, but he was *still* fucking with her. She didn't understand why he didn't just let go and really move on with his life. Find someone else to take the crap that he came with. Emerson reached and squeezed Mikayla's arm affectionately.

"Well, when he finally does, we will be right here to celebrate with you. In the meantime, I want you to just enjoy your life. That sorry motherfucker took enough of it away from you and he's still trying to, but fuck him. With all this stuff going on with your mom especially."

"All of this is a little much, but I tell you what I am going to do. I'm going to finish my drink, go home to my girls, and continue on with my life."

With that, Mikayla downed the rest of her drink and set her glass on the table. Emerson and Charlie followed suit.

Emerson checked her watch and saw that it was almost four o'clock. She figured it was time to head on home. They paid for their drinks and left the bar. Mikayla had driven, so they rode with her back to her house and went home from there.

It felt good to have everything out in the open with her friends. Well, almost everything.

When Emerson pulled up to her home, there was Jeep Wrangler in the driveway. A little buzzed, she smiled to herself when she got out of her Mercedes. The front door was already unlocked, and sitting on the couch, seemingly waiting for someone, was a woman in her mid-twenties. She was very pretty, with an almond-colored complexion and hazel eyes. She was slim-thick with a large ass behind her.

When Emerson entered, the young woman instantly stood up and walked toward her.

"Hey, Cali," Emerson said to her.

"Hey, baby," Cali responded and kissed Emerson on the lips.

Her tongue slid through, and she deeply kissed Emerson right there in the foyer of the house. Emerson's buzz already had her senses tingling, and now her clit had been awakened. Emerson's hands slid up to Cali's perky C cups and pinched her nipples through her clothes.

"You miss me?" Cali asked when she broke the kiss.

"Of course," Emerson replied, and Cali made a face.

"You've been drinking. I smell it all over your breath."

"I went to grab a drink with my girls. That's all," Emerson said, moving around her and going for the kitchen. "Mikayla found out her mother was murdered today."

"Oh, no!" Cali said, looking genuinely concerned. "That's terrible. Do they know who did it?"

"No, not yet. But there is a detective working the case."

"How is Mikayla doing with it all? I know it has to be tough."

"Honestly, I think she's sad, but they didn't have much of a relationship. In fact, they didn't have a relationship at all. Mikayla was in foster care when she was a kid. Her mom pretty much chose the streets over her kids."

"That's sad," Cali said with a frown.

"It's life," Emerson told her, taking her hand. "Lets go into the bedroom. I want to see that pretty face of yours between my legs."

Cali licked her lips seductively and headed for the room.

The thing with Cali wasn't supposed to happen, but it did. They'd met at an event Emerson was hosting, and they hit it off. She was someone that Emerson could laugh with, cuddle, and sex all she wanted without having to worry about strings being attached. Cali wasn't openly gay, but when prompted, she had no shame in saying she was interested in women sexually.

At first Emerson was apprehensive about dealing with another woman. Macy had done a number on her. But Cali was a person who valued her private life as well, so it put Emerson's mind at ease. The sex was so spontaneous and explosive that Emerson was hooked. Also, the world already knew Emerson had been involved with a woman before. What was one more?

Chapter 7

Damian

Most people didn't go to the club on a Thursday, but Damian wasn't most people. He sat in a corner seat, enjoying the nude women dancing on poles around the place. The lights were low, setting the seductive tone for the girls, and for Damian, it provided the perfect mask. See, he wasn't there to get his dick sucked by one of the whores. He was there on a mission—a mission named Johnny Bucks.

Johnny was a high roller in Baltimore and didn't care to hide that he was rolling in dough. When Damian found out that he would be in Sphinx that night, he jumped at the chance to rob him. Since he'd gotten out of jail, things had been hard for him. It didn't matter that the crime happened so long ago or that he was a child when it did. No one wanted to hire a felon, so from time to time, he did what he had to do. The money he'd gotten from Mikayla had held him over for a while, but since he had to split it with his mom, it was gone within a year. Jewel had been blowing his phone up, saying that they needed to get in touch with Mikayla again to get some more money, and Damian couldn't agree more. That was how he ended up back in Baltimore.

For the past two years, Damian resided in Atlanta. Jewel visited him sometimes, but for the most part, they spoke over the phone. She was the only person he trusted in the world. Lately, however, she'd been a little hard to reach. It had been two weeks since he'd heard from her before she called about the money.

The plan was they would meet with Mikayla Friday evening and blackmail her into giving them another hundred thousand dollars. Damian had been keeping up with her. She was doing big things, and to him, that meant bigger money. In the meantime, Damian didn't see the harm in getting a few more coins. When he overheard a few women in the liquor store earlier say that they were so excited for Johnny Bucks to come into the club that night, he took it as a sign from above. Why have a little when he could have a lot?

Johnny needed to tighten up on security, because his people were drinking and enjoying the festivities just like him. When Johnny got up to head to the bathroom, he took his book bag of money with him. Nobody followed after him, and Damian knew it was his time to make his move.

"Move," he said, and pushed the woman giving him a lap dance to the side.

"You broke motherfucker!"

The dark chocolate woman with blond hair spat at him, but he didn't care. He left her standing there while he followed after Damian. When he was out of the main floor and in a hallway that had red carpet, he rested his hand on his waist. His hand wrapped around the butt of his gun as he crept. Right when he was on the bathroom door, he saw a movement out of the corner of his eye. He whipped his head to the right, and sure enough, there was someone leaning on the wall and flipping a coin. It was a man dressed in a tailored suit and rocking a fresh tapered fade.

"I wouldn't do that if I were you," the man said.

"Do what, take a piss?" Damian feigned ignorance.

"You and I both know why you were going into that bathroom. And it wasn't to take nobody's piss, Damian."

The man flipped the coin one more time and caught it before he pushed off the wall. Damian was caught off guard by the fact that the guy knew his name when Damian hadn't seen him a day in his life. He tried to pull his gun, but the man in the suit shook a finger his way.

"I wouldn't do that either," he said. "Tonight's lesson is going to be wise decisions. I'm going to skip right to the chase, Damian. You owe me."

"Owe you? Motherfucka, I don't even know you. How the fuck do you know my name?"

"As I said, you owe me," the man repeated himself. "And robbing a drug dealer at gunpoint in a strip club just isn't a wise decision. I don't need you in jail. Within the next hour, you're going to find out some life-altering news. You're going to be angry, and you're going to want to murder the world. But you're not going to. What you're going to do is call this number." The man reached in his pocket, pulled out a card, and handed it to Damian.

Damian snatched it and tried to make sense of what was just said to him. It sounded like a bunch of bullshit, but still, he wanted the guy to elaborate. Especially since he knew his name.

"How do you know who I am, man?" Damian said and looked back up. "And what do you me—"

The man was gone. It was like he had vanished into thin air. Damian spun around in a circle to cover all angles with his eyes. In the meantime, Johnny Bucks had exited the bathroom and was looking at Damian like he was out of his mind.

"Aye, you all right?"

Damian turned to Johnny and wished he could knock him out, but by then Johnny's security had come to find him.

"Johnny, everything cool?" the big, buff man asked, eyeing Damian down.

"Yeah, shit is straight. I was just making sure homie was good. I think all this pussy fucking his mind up," Johnny said with a laugh. "That's all right, though. More for me! Aye, bruh, keep your head up."

With that, Johnny walked away with Damian's lick. However, Damian had almost forgotten about why he was even there in the first place. He felt like he was losing his mind, and if it weren't for the piece of paper in his hand, he wouldn't have believed the encounter happened. He would have just blamed it on the alcohol.

He figured he would just call it a night and head back to the hotel he was staying in. Jewel would call him in the morning and haul him to breakfast like she always did. Then she would fuss about how buff he'd gotten and tell him to slow down on the weights. He wondered how much she was thinking they could get from that dear sister of his that time. It would have to be something to hold him over for a while.

In his pocket, he felt his phone begin to ring as he walked out of the club and to his car. When he finally pulled it out to see who was calling him so late, he stopped in his tracks. It was Mikayla. Had he thought her up?

"What's up?" he answered in a smug tone.

"Damian? Damian, is that you?" Mikayla asked, sounding unsure.

"You called my phone, didn't you?"

"Well, the first two numbers I tried were disconnected," Mikayla said and then paused.

"I move around a lot. To what do I owe this call?"

"I was calling to talk about what happened."

"What happened?"

"The detective didn't call you?"

"Detective?" Damian asked. "What the fuck would a detective be doing calling my phone?"

"You haven't heard. Oh my God. Damian, I'm so sorry. It's about Jewel."

"What about her?"

"She's . . . Damian, she's dead. They found her body last night."

"You're lying."

"I swear to you I'm not. I had to identify her body."

Damian felt the blood drain from his face. Suddenly, he thought back to what the man said, and he had been right. Damian wanted to murder everybody.

"What happened?" he asked in a monotone.

"She was murdered. They think somebody tortured her. They said that the way her body was, it looked like whatever whoever did it to her wanted, wanted it bad."

"So what do you want to do about it?" Damian asked, forgetting who he was talking to.

"The detective said that they're handling it the best that they can. Right now, all I'm focused on is the funeral arrangements. Where are you?"

"I–I'm in Baltimore actually."

"You're here? Wait, if you're here already and didn't even know Jewel was dead, why *are* you here? *Both* of you were here." realization dawned in Mikayla's voice, and she gave a spiteful scoff. "You two were coming to see me, weren't you?"

Damien was quiet. He was still trying to grasp the news that Jewel was dead. Murdered. Who would want to murder her? Damian knew that she was involved in some unethical dealings, but it was never enough to make him feel like she was in danger.

"I knew it," Mikayla continued. "You were coming to ask for some more money, weren't you? Huh? You two were going to try to blackmail me again? Well, I have news for you, nigga. I ain't giving you shit ever again, so you can chalk it up. You made the choice to do the time, and regardless of if you were the one inside, I was never free. I'll give you a call tomorrow so you can meet me and discuss arrangements."

She hung up before Damian could retort. He wouldn't have had anything to say anyways, however. He was stuck. Jewel was dead. He kept replaying those three words over and over in his head and trying to make himself believe them. He didn't know Mikayla that well, but he knew her well enough to know she wouldn't lie about something so serious.

Standing outside his Cadillac CTS he shoved his hands in his pockets and hung his head. "Mama," he whispered. The fingers on his right hand brushed against the piece of paper he'd placed in his pocket absentmindedly while on the phone. He pulled it out and stared at the number scribbled there. There were so many thoughts going through his mind, and the person that gave him the card was one of them.

Before he knew it, his phone was back to his ear. The sound of the ringing seemed to go on forever before there was finally an answer.

"I told you that you'd be calling me."

"Who are you? And how did you know my mother was dead?" Damian asked, finally getting into his car.

"People call me The Bone Collector," the man said. "But that's too long for my taste. You can just call me Bone. I am a man who collect debts."

"What does you collecting debts have to do with my mother?"

"You see, Damian, I work for someone very powerful, and Jewel took something very valuable from him. A rare pink diamond worth one million dollars, but to the owner, it's priceless. When we finally caught up to her, one of our men got a little too . . . *inventive* with her. She died because she wouldn't tell us where the diamond is."

"Your boss had my mother killed?" Damian asked. "Who is he?"

"Someone who is as private as a ghost. Tyrant."

"And you're telling me this so boldly like I'm not gonna—"

"Find me and force me to give up my boss's location before you kill me?" Bone yawned. "I've heard all of that before, and guess where those men are? Dead. Some dismembered. Now, let me remind you that Jewel made the first move. A stupid one. And now you're left to pay the price. You are either going to come up with the money or the diamond. And boy, do I strongly suggest it be the diamond."

"And why would I do anything for your boss after he murdered my mother?"

"Because we know about Braxton."

Damian's heart stopped when he heard the mention of his son's name. No one knew about him, not even Jewel. Braxton had been conceived with a stripper on a drunken night shortly after Damian got out of jail. If it weren't for the DNA test he had done, he wouldn't have believed he even had a son. He didn't think he could love anyone so much, but Braxton didn't just have his heart. He *was* his heart. Damian didn't know how Bone knew about Braxton, but he felt the goosebumps form on his arms.

"He's just a boy," was all he could get out.

"We don't give a fuck. The only thing that matters is that there is a debt that needs to be paid. As long as you pay it, little Braxton will live to see his second birthday. You have sixty days. And Damian?"

"What?" Damian growled.

"I'll send you a photo of what the diamond looks like. And remember, we'll be watching you."

Click.

Shortly after the call disconnected, a text message came through. Damian threw his phone to the ground with a loud yell. He smacked himself in the forehead a few times. The world seemed so small at that second. But he would do anything to keep his son safe. He had to find that diamond.

Chapter 8

Mason

"This case is putting a thorn in my ass," Mason groaned and tossed a folder on his desk.

He'd been in the field for two days straight with barely any home time since he'd gotten the call from Detective Lawson. The first day, he'd gone straight to the scene of the crime, and he saw the body before they took it away. It was probably the second most gory thing Mason had seen in all of his days as law enforcement.

The people in the apartment next to the murder scene said at one point they heard someone shout, "Where is it?" But that was all they had to go on. That day, Mason was back in the office to see if anyone had found out anything. Ever since the murder of Jewel had gone public, they'd been getting all types of anonymous tips that led nowhere.

"Tell me about it. I just got a call from a lady that swears that the murderer is her dead son reincarnated," Lawson said. "She swears she saw him do the same thing to her cat when he was alive."

"Lawson, people are crazy," Mason said, shaking his head. "I wish the media didn't release the information about the state of her body. Besides the crazy cat lady, have you heard anything else?"

"No, not yet," Lawson said. "But I'm going to go inter-view a few more tenants later today."

"That's a good idea."

Lawson started to leave his office but turned around at the door. "I noticed that you haven't left your office since you've been here. You want some of this meat loaf I brought with me?"

"Meat loaf? Woman, you are going to make someone an honest man one day. You always come in here with homecooked meals."

"What can I say? I love to eat. That's why I have to work so hard in the gym." Lawson laughed.

"Nothing wrong with it. I'll take you up on that offer another time. My girl packed me a lunch. You go over and talk to the tenants. I want to go through some of these forensic photos."

Mason ignored the longing in her gaze. She stood there for a few more moments before she left. Lawson was a young but good detective. She cared about her job, but more importantly, she cared about helping others. Mason just hoped she would keep her obvious infatuation uder control. Although he wasn't a married man, he was in a committed relationship.

Charlie was more than enough woman for him and then some. She had become his family when she bore him his first child. He loved her more than she could ever know. The bond they shared was one he'd never had before, so he would never do anything to jeopardize it, especially something as foolish as messing around in the workplace. Lawson was a good-looking woman, Mason would give her that. But she just wasn't Charlie.

He continued to sift through the folder of photos of the crime scene and at the same time recount his own memory of it. He hated that he felt like he'd missed something. He stared closely at the pictures and examined every inch of them, no matter how horrible the photograph. He came across one of the ground by Jewel's feet. Blood had been splattered everywhere, and a few of Jewel's fingers were on the floor. Mason's eyes fell on her hand, hanging by the leg of the chair she was sitting in. She was missing a total of three fingers, and Mason didn't want to imagine the pain that came with that.

"Wait, what's that?" he said to himself.

Behind her hand and etched into the wooden chair leg was some sort of marking. He shuffled through the photos until he found one that was zoomed in on her hand, but gave the perfect angle on the symbol. Mason instantly took notice of the wooden shavings next to each marking. It was fresh. That wasn't what was taking Mason on a ride. The fact that he'd seen that symbol before was. He jumped up from his desk and hurried over to his case file cabinet. He pulled out a drawer and fingered through the files until he found the one he was looking for.

The Bennett case.

A year ago, a body had turned up in an old loading dock. The body had been so badly burned that they had to use dental records to identify the body. It was the worst scene Mason had ever seen. The man's name was Walter Bennett. On the ground next to his body there had been a symbol spraypainted on the ground. Nobody had thought anything of it then because there were a lot of spray-painted numbers and symbols around the dock. But now, Mason was thinking that maybe he should have dug a little deeper.

He found the photo he was looking for and took it back to his desk to compare.

"Shit," he said out loud.

The symbols were the same—the number three with four dots around it. How could he have missed that? He remembered that Walter left behind a wife. Mason had spoken to her a few times following the murder. The case was still open, in fact. They never caught the person who did it. He quickly took two photos of the symbols side by side with his phone and sent them in a text. Afterward, he called the person he'd just sent them to.

"Donald Pollard speaking." Mason's good friend answered the phone.

Mason had known Don since high school, and the two had done well at keeping in touch. Don was a black man who had been born with a silver spoon and had started a few companies right out of high school. In his spare time, Don liked to buy, sell, and trade rare artifacts. He sometimes did business with some very bad people. Nothing illegal, so he said; however, he had access to the underground world in Baltimore that Mason couldn't get close to on his own. He had access to information.

"Don, it's Mason. Did you get my texts?"

"Yep, just did," Don told him. "I'm trying to figure out what the hell I'm looking at, though."

"That's the thing—I don't know. And I need you to find out."

"Mason, I—"

"Hey, you still owe me from covering for you last Thanksgiving. I *still* don't know why you were late, but Clarissa thinks you were with me. But maybe, just maybe, I remember where I really was and should tell her—"

"All right, all right! You've made your point, man. And for your information, I was doing some volunteer work with the homeless that day."

"Yeah, yeah. So, are you gonna help me or what?"

"I'll send you over what I find," Don told him. "Next time, this kind of information is gonna cost you."

"Thanks," Mason said and disconnected the call.

He closed the file in his hands and grabbed his coat. He had a widow across town to go talk to.

Mason knocked on the front door of a nice two-story home. The light in the front room was on, so he stood back and waited for someone to answer. When he heard someone approaching the door, he stood up a little straighter.

A brown-skinned woman with curly hair poked her head out. She looked to be in her thirties, but her file said that she was pushing fifty. "Can I help you?" she asked skeptically.

"Loretta Bennett?"

"Yes. Who's asking?"

Mason reached in his coat, pulled out his badge, and flashed it at her. "My name is Mason Dayle."

"Yeah, I remember you. You're that detective who talked to me after Wallie died."

"That's actually why I'm here."

"You caught the person who did it?" she asked hopefully.

"No, I'm sorry, we haven't. But we are still working on it. I just need to ask you some follow-up questions."

"Follow-up questions after a year?"

"Sometimes these things can take time," he told her. "Can I come in?"

Loretta looked him up and down before rolling her eyes. She sighed and opened the door wide enough for him to come in.

Mason hadn't been to her house. The last time he had to question her, she came down to the station. It had a homey vibe to it, and all of her and Walter's pictures were still on the walls. Mason took notice of one in particular of Walter standing on a boat.

"I was in the kitchen when you knocked. You can come on in there," Loretta said and led the way.

She had been in the middle of breading some catfish filets. The smell of the seasoning was awakening his tastebuds, and Mason knew it was going to be delicious when it was done.

They sat down at the kitchen table, and Loretta crossed her hands while looking at him. "So, what's this about, detective?" she asked, smoothing out her apron.

"I just wanted to ask you some questions about your husband that I didn't ask before," Mason said, pulling out a small notepad and pen. "Like, did he have any habits or hobbies?"

"I think everybody knew that Wallie was into gambling. He used to win big, so it was a hobby turned into a habit, I guess you can say."

"Unh-huh," Mason said, jotting something down in his notepad.

At that moment, he felt his phone vibrate in his pocket. When he grabbed it, he saw that it was Don giving him a call back, and he placed his pen down.

"Give me a moment, please, Mrs. Bennett." He excused himself from the kitchen. He answered the phone in the hallway, hoping for good news. "Don, tell me you found something."

"I did, but I don't think you're going to like what you hear," Don answered. "The symbol belongs to Tyrant."

"Who the fuck is Tyrant, Don?"

"He's a loan shark and a motherfucka that you don't want to fuck with, that's who. Half the people I asked didn't want anything to do with my questions," Don said.

"They're scared of him?"

"Try terrified. And they have good reason to be. The dude is sick. Whoever doesn't pay their debt to him turns up dead in the most horrific ways. When it's done, his symbol is left behind as a warning to his other clients."

"Why hasn't he ever been arrested if people know who is committing all of these sick murders?"

"Because Tyrant is just an alias. Nobody knows his real name. Nobody even knows what he looks like. They say he wears a leather mask when deals go down."

"So he's a professional. When you don't pay him back, you don't know *who* it is looking for you."

"Bingo. And from the sounds of it, he does business all over. The guy is like a walking bank. But that's not all I found out."

"What's the rest?"

"If this is the guy responsible for those two photos you sent me, you don't want to go looking for him. The last detectives who did that are still missing."

"Thanks for the warning, but I ain't scared of no ghost," Mason told him and looked over his shoulder to make sure he was still alone. "Thanks, man. Good work. I gotta go."

He hung up the phone and went back into the kitchen. Loretta was still in the same seat, waiting patiently.

"I'm sorry about that," he told her. "Where were we?" He sat down.

"No problem. I was telling you about Wallie's gambling."

"Right. Is that how he was able to afford that diamond Patek watch?"

"Huh?"

"In the photo you have hanging in your living room, the one of Walter standing on the boat, your husband is wearing a fifty thousand–dollar watch."

"Oh," Loretta said, looking genuinely shocked. "Well I—I guess. I don't know. How would *you* know how much his watch is?"

"I wanted one just like it, but unfortunately, it was out of my budget," he told her with a smile. "Is there anything, anything at all, that you can remember that you might not have told us back then?"

"No. I told you guys everything important."

"What about details that you think we might not care about?"

"Umm," Loretta said, looking as if she were in deep thought. "Well, around the time that it all happened, Wallie started acting real strange."

"Strange like how?"

"Well, he was irritated and angry all the time. I thought it was because he wasn't hitting with his gambling. Then he started getting really jumpy. Anytime anyone would *breathe,* it was like the man would dang near jump out of his socks. He just kept trying to convince me that we needed to move. He said it wasn't safe anymore, something about tyrants coming to our house."

"What?"

"That's exactly what I said! We live in a good area. We have neighborhood watch!"

"No, that's not what I meant. Did you say Tyrant?"

"Yeah, he kept going on and on about them. Saying that we were going to lose everything. I kept telling him that nobody was going to rob us."

"And that's not what *he* meant," Mason said. "Mrs. Bennett, did Walter ever borrow money?"

"H—how did you know about that?" Loretta asked.

"Please just answer the question."

"Yes, he did. Once. Thirty thousand dollars for the down payment for this house. He had been promising me a house for years, but even together we didn't have enough. Not for what we wanted anyway. He said the guy he was borrowing from was legit and had the cash on hand. He told me not to worry because it was only one time, and he could pay the money back in installments. We paid it back fast, and it was only one time."

"Are you sure about that?"

"I think so," she said, not looking too confident in her words. "I mean, I speculated that he might have done it again. He did a lot of nice things for me that were costly, but he always promised me they were just his winnings. Tell me what you're thinking?"

"I'm thinking that your husband *did* borrow more money regularly. That he didn't think anything of it because he did hit big. However, when his winnings started dwindling down, so did the payments on his loans. I'm thinking that's why he was acting jumpy in the end there. He knew someone was after him."

"You think the person who he borrowed money from killed him?"

"Either he did it himself, or he had somebody do it for him."

"Well, arrest him then!"

"Can't." Mason sighed. "I wish it were that easy, but the person I think your husband borrowed money from goes by the name Tyrant, which isn't his real name. That's the bad thing about doing these kinds of deals. You never know who you're really dealing with."

"Oh, my poor Wallie," Loretta said sadly. "Maybe if I didn't enjoy the finer things in life so much, he wouldn't have felt the need to do all that."

"Thank you for your cooperation today, Mrs. Bennett," Mason said, getting up from the table. "You've been a real help to me."

"You're welcome, detective. If you find the monster who did that horrible thing to my husband, I better be the first to know."

"You have my word," Mason said and bid her farewell.

On the way back to his car, there were only two thoughts going on in his head: finding out more about Tyrant the loan shark, and finding out what business he had with Jewel.

Chapter 9

Mikayla

It had been a couple of days since talking to Damian on the phone, but the two of them had agreed to meet that Sunday afternoon. Mikayla woke up early and took her time getting ready that day. She remembered the last time she'd seen her brother and couldn't believe that she ever even thought about mending the relationship. Both he and Jewel had been back to extort her, and there she was about to pay for her funeral.

The girls were going to be staying home with the babysitter while she was out. That was good, because Mikayla had made the decision to bring a gun. She didn't trust Damian, and the way Jewel was found, Mikayla had no clue what kind of stuff they were into. All she wanted to do was bury the woman and be done with them forever.

"Bye, Mommy!" Kai shouted and ran down the hallway when she saw Mikayla exit her room. "Are you about to go look at coffins for Grandma?"

"Grandma?" Mikayla asked, raising her eyebrow. "When did you start calling her that?"

"I mean, she is my grandma." Kai shrugged before giving her mom a hug. "I love you. If you need us, we're here."

Mikayla was touched by her daughter's sympathetic gesture. Mikayla didn't want to put her in grown folks' business by telling her that she wasn't down and out about it, because then she would have to explain why, and that would just take too much time. Instead, she just kissed her baby girl on her forehead and returned the hug.

"Thanks, kid. I wonder where you got your sweetness from."

"Probably you," Kai told her before pulling away and running back to her room.

Mikayla walked to Zuri's closed bedroom door and knocked on it before she opened it. Just like she thought, Zuri was still knocked out asleep, and it was almost ten o'clock. The sun was peeking through her blinds, but to Zuri it probably still felt like nighttime, since the covers were over her head. Mikayla pulled them back and shook her daughter's shoulder until her eyes blinked open.

"Zuri, Angela is here to keep you guys. She's making breakfast," Mikayla said.

"Okay, Mommy," Zuri said in a groggy voice. "You leaving?"

"Yes. I'm on my way out the door."

"You look nice," she said with a yawn. "What kind of casket are you going to pick? I think she would have liked a pink one."

"I'm not even sure if we're going to get a casket, honey."

"Because she didn't have life insurance?"

"How do you know anything about life insurance?" Mikayla was amused.

"I saw something about it on TV. It's when you die and an insurance company pays your family thousands of dollars. If you made your payments anyway."

"You really know your stuff," Mikayla said, kissing her cheek. "And no, she did not have life insurance. I have to meet with the detective today, and then I'm going over to the funeral home."

"If she didn't have life insurance, can't you just pay for it, Mommy? Haven't you been making a ton of money now? Your face is on a billboard. She should be buried."

"There are a lot of things that you don't understand. And I don't want you to worry your pretty little head about them either. What I want you to do is go on downstairs and see what goodies Angela cooked up for you girls. Take your sister."

Mikayla watched her get out of bed and put on her plush pink unicorn robe before leaving the room. She went downstairs and gave Angela a list of things that needed to be done around the house before she left. She didn't eat anything, because Detective Janes had asked her to meet him at a little low-key eatery.

On the way there, she wondered if there had been any kind of break in the case. She knew it was still early, and those kinds of things took time, but still, she hoped that maybe he had *something*.

When she pulled into the parking lot of the eatery, she saw the detective through the window of the restaurant, already seated. She hurried inside and waved a hand his way before making her way over. He stood to greet her.

"I'm sorry I'm a little late," she said with a smile. "I woke up early and everything. I don't know what happened."

"Sometimes when we have a little extra time on our hands, we get a little besides ourselves," Detective Janes said, flashing her a brilliantly white smile. "No harm, no foul."

Mikayla took in the man in front of her. She didn't remember him being so good looking. From his fresh haircut to the designer shoes on his feet, he was delectable. She liked the way his full lips moved when he talked. It put her in the mind of Michael B. Jordan. The gray suit he wore was fitted, and when he shook her hand, a diamond watch flashed from under the sleeve of his suit jacket.

She got a grip on herself before she started to drool, and pointed at the booth he was sitting in. He had a folder and papers out on the table already.

"Shall we get to it then?" she asked.

"Of course," he said, and the two of them sat down. He handed her a menu. "Hungry?"

"Starving," she said, looking at the food on the laminated menu. "I think I'm going to have a burger, but just don't tell my friends. We're supposed to be staying clear of red meat."

"Your secret is safe with me, Mrs. King," he said with a smile.

"I hate that."

"You hate what?"

"That people still have to call me Mrs. King," she said with a sigh. "My husband won't sign the divorce papers. It's like I'm stuck in a nightmare."

"I'm sorry about that," Detective Janes said, sounding genuine.

"Don't be. It's not your fault," she said, pushing her menu to the middle. "So, what are you going to have?"

"I think I'm going to follow the leader here and get a burger too," he said and called the waiter over.

After placing their orders, he looked back at her. "I guess we can get some of the business out of the way while they're making our food."

"Yes, we can. Do you guys know any more about what happened?"

"We have some people working the case, but we don't have much more than what we did the other day," he said. "I was actually hoping you could help me out a little bit."

"Help you out how?"

"Do you know anybody your mother might have been with? Any friends, or maybe lovers?"

"No." She shook her head. "I didn't know much about her. We weren't close. I didn't even know she was in Baltimore."

"Really?" The detective's eyebrows shot up in surprise. "She's been living here for the past three months. You mean to tell me you didn't know that?"

"*Living* here?" Mikayla was shocked, and she looked back at him with disbelief all over her face. "No, I had no clue. Are you sure?"

"Yes. The lease agreement we found in her apartment goes back three months."

"So that was her apartment that she was found in," Mikayla said and shook her head. None of it was making sense. She knew Damian lived out of state, and she just assumed Jewel was close to him. Why had she moved back to Baltimore ?

"When was the last time you saw your mother?"

"A few years ago," Mikayla told him and noticed his puzzled face. "Once again, we weren't close. When I *did* live with her, she wasn't much of a mother. I grew up in foster care because she couldn't get her shit together."

"Your file here says that you have a brother," he said. "Did he go to foster care too?"

"Yes," Mikayla said, fidgeting a little.

"It also says here that he went to prison for murdering your foster father."

"Yes, he did. But that's all in the past now," Mikayla said, trying to brush past the topic. "He was a kid when it happened. He paid his debt to society."

"So you two must be close then."

"Why do you say that?"

"Because of the way you just defended him. You two aren't close?"

"No, but not because I didn't want to be," Mikayla said, choosing her words wisely. "Sometimes life is crueler

to some. And sometimes once you cross that line, there
is no coming back. But we aren't here to talk about my
family drama."

"All right," he said, recognizing the hint in her tone.
"Mrs. King, do you know anyone that might want to kill
Jewel?"

"I don't know." Mikayla shrugged her shoulders. "But
the way she moved, probably a lot of people. My mom
dwasn't a good person, detective. Let's be very clear on
that. The only reason I'm even agreeing to bury her is
because *somebody* has to."

"Because you're a good woman," he said, looking at
her. That time, she recognize the look in his eyes. "Tell
me something. You're beautiful, and from this piece of
paper, I see that you're also a smart businesswoman.
Why would a man want to divorce you?"

"Divorce me?" Mikayla put a hand to her chest. "Oh, no,
honey. You have it backwards. I'm divorcing *him*."

"Why? If you don't mind me asking."

"Because he couldn't keep his hands to himself,"
Mikayla said without batting a lash. "He treated me like
shit. No, he treated me like a doormat in the winter that
you wiped your boots on after a muddy day in the snow."

"Damn." He shook his head. "I don't know what's
wrong with our brothas not being able to keep their
hands to themselves. I'm glad you got out with your life.
Some don't have that luxury."

"Thank God for that." Mikayla nodded.

The waiter brought back their drinks and shortly after
that, their food. As they ate, she asked him a few more
questions about the case.

"So, do you guys think that it was someone she knew?"

"It's a good possibility. There was no sign of forced en-
try, and even a few drink glasses out. She either knew the
person or expected them. Her apartment was ransacked.

When you *were* around your mother, do you remember her having anything valuable?"

"She had a thing for jewelry," Mikayla said, remembering her mother. "The guys she dated would buy her nice necklaces and rings. She was particularly into diamonds. One guy got her a rock so big I thought it would break her finger. She would always end up pawning the jewelry. I doubt she could hold onto something worth some value for more than five minutes."

"We're just trying to figure out what they were looking for," he said. "The place was flipped upside down."

Mikayla checked the time on her phone and hurried to finish her food. She'd told Damian to meet her at the funeral home at around noon. The last thing she needed was for him to think she was a no show. She thought about the gun she had under her seat in her car and hoped she wouldn't have to use it. When she was finished eating, she pulled out her wallet to pay.

"I got it," Detective Janes told her.

"You sure?"

"Of course I'm sure. It's not every day I get to have lunch with someone as pretty as you."

"Yeah, right," Mikayla said, trying not to smile too hard. "With looks like those, you probably have a whole pack of women chasing after you."

"A whole pack?" He laughed heartily. "I didn't know women came in packs. But if they did, I can assure you that I don't have one chasing me. In fact, I'm more single than a Pringle, or whatever these kids are saying these days."

"Well, Mr. Single Pringle, we'll have to do this again sometime," she told him.

"You can call me Brandon, and I'd like that very much. Next time, I'll take you to a spot a little more romantic than this."

"Romance already?" she asked, batting her eyelashes.

"Romance forever," he said with a wink.

"I'll remember you said that," she said and started for the door. "I'll be waiting for your phone call."

She had the dopiest smile on her face the whole walk to the car. How had meeting him for a murder case turned into them agreeing to go on a date? The world was a crazy place, but Mikayla was used to that. She told herself that she was going to hold on to her good mood all day. Nobody was going to ruin it, not even Damian.

When she got to the funeral home, the first thing she noticed was the newer cherry red Cadillac parked in the parking lot. It stood out to her, and she wondered if Damian was inside it. She parked on the other side of the parking lot, close to the entrance, and took her phone out of her purse. She scrolled on it until she found the number she'd been calling to reach him. She pressed dial and listened to it ring three times before he answered.

"Is that you in the Cadillac?"

"I guess I'm not as inconspicuous as I thought." His gruff voice came through from the other end.

"Not at all. You stick out like a sore thumb," she said and reached under her seat. "Well, I'm about to go inside. There's a little area where we can sit and talk about everything before we make any decisions."

"Cool."

Mikayla hung up and tossed her phone in her tote. She then made sure that her pistol was on safety before she slid it inside the bag as well. She got out of the car and went inside the funeral home.

"Mrs. King! Nice to see you again."

Mikayla was greeted by the mortician, Mr. Carpenter, a stocky black man with a thick mustache. He was just a little taller than Mikayla and a lot more wide. Mikayla had never buried anyone before, but after shopping around, she'd come across Carpenter's Funeral Home, and out of everyone, he was the one she felt wasn't just after her money.

When she entered, he'd been in the middle of looking through the drawers of the front desk. She nodded her head in greeting to him.

"Mr. Carpenter, my brother and I are here to figure out what we want to do," she said, motioning toward the door behind her. "I'm just waiting for him to come in so we can sit down and discuss some stuff."

"Finding it tough to decide between cremation and a burial still?"

"Something like that," she said. "That's just a big chunk of money to be spending out of nowhere."

Especially on someone I don't like, she finished in her head.

The door to the funeral home opened, and she knew who was behind her before she turned her head. Damian stood there, tall and dark, the way she remembered him. His beard and mustache were neatly trimmed like he had just done it that day. He wore his hair in a low fade, and he had a lost look in his eyes when they connected with hers.

Suddenly, Mikayla felt a sadness so strong overwhelm her that she almost hugged him. It was like they were children all over again, and all she wanted to do was protect him. She thought about how he must have felt. He didn't have Jewel for very long as a child, and now here he was, only two years free and she was gone.

"Hey, Damian," she said.

"Hey, Mikayla," he said back.

Mr. Carpenter looked from one sibling to the other, because you could cut the tension with a knife. Finally, when nobody made a move, he cleared his throat.

"You two are welcome to use our waiting area to discuss anything you need to," he said and pointed to an area with four chairs and a table. "Just holler for me when you need me. I'll be here."

Mikayla led the way to the chairs, and she and Damian sat across from each other. He seemed put together almost, but there was something underneath the surface that she couldn't figure out—*how* had he been put together? She was sure the money he'd gotten from her was long gone. She wondered what kind of job he had, or how he was making ends meet. She didn't even know why she was wondering that. Maybe it was the big sister in her.

"So, what do you need me here for? Money?" Damian asked. "Because I'll be the first to tell you that I ain't got it right now."

"And I'll be the first to tell you that I already figured that."

"Okay, then we come back to my first question. Why am I here?"

"Because you were closer to her than me," Mikayla told him truthfully. "I figured you'd want to take part in the final goodbyes."

"Well, how thoughtful. You probably want me to help you decide if we should cremate her or bury her," he said sarcastically. But when Mikayla gave him a look that told him that was exactly what she wanted, he was shocked. "Wow. I know shit's fucked up between us all, but she still deserves to be buried. Don't you want her to have a place you can go visit?"

"I don't really care, honestly. Why would I? The last thing she was planning to do was take from me. "

"You will," he said, looking her dead in the eye. "One day, you will."

"Well, she didn't have life insurance. It will be cheaper to cremate her."

"We don't have to have a funeral for her. Just you and me is enough. That should cut the cost down, right?"

She could see that he was adamant about not having Jewel cremated. She was so angry, but more at herself than anyone else, because even when she was done wrong, she found herself doing for others. It was a gift and a curse.

"Fine," she said with a sigh. "Let's call Mr. Carpenter back in here so I can get the costs of everything."

It took all of an hour for burial arrangements to be made for Jewel. Damian didn't make it clear how long he would be in town, but Mikayla figured the faster the better. The burial would take place in two days, on Tuesday.

When they were all done, Mikayla thanked Mr. Carpenter for all of his help and left the funeral home. When she was almost to her car, Damian shouted her name. She turned around to see him jogging toward her.

"Hey, Mikayla, wait."

"What?" she asked.

"Uh . . ." He rubbed the back of his head. "I wasn't expecting to be in town past tonight, and . . ."

"And you don't have any place to stay?" Mikayla asked incredulously. "You and this woman came here to—"

"Talk you into giving us some more money. I know," Damian huffed. "She was only doing it for me. You might not understand since you have the perfect life, but times have been hard. I can't get a job because nobody will hire a felon. She didn't like seeing me like that. I know you don't want to believe it, but she changed. She wasn't the same person we grew up with, and she was clean. From everything."

"Then how did she end up where she's at?"

"I don't know, but I'm going to find out," he said firmly. "But I need somewhere to lay my head. I know you have the room. That's the least you can do for me."

"I already gave you a hundred thousand dollars."

"Okay, the second least thing you can do for me," he said with a smirk, but got serious again. "Please."

Mikayla groaned at the thought of Damian being in her house. All of the questions that would come with his presence were already giving her a headache, and they hadn't even been asked yet. The girls would want to know why she never talked about her brother. She would have to think of an answer fast because before she knew it, Damian was in his Cadillac, following her to her house.

Chapter 10

Charlie

She had been dreaming about being on a boat in Paris when she felt herself get shaken awake. When she opened her eyes, she saw MJ standing there in his pajamas, wide awake at the side of her bed. He must have climbed out of his crib again. Charlie wouldn't have believed that it was nine o'clock in the morning if she hadn't seen it on her digital clock. She sat up in bed and stretched big.

"Hey, Poo Poo," she said and looked at her son fondly. "You want to eat?"

MJ nodded his head and climbed in bed with his mom. He sat cuddled in her lap, and she embraced him, engulfing him in all her warmth. After a few moments, she kissed his forehead and got out of bed with him in her arms.

"You want some toast and oatmeal?" she asked him. "I'm sure you'll get a snack when you get to daycare. You know Miss Melinda loves her some you. Don't tell the other kids, but I think you're her favorite."

MJ smiled as Charlie talked to him. She always talked to him, even though he couldn't give good conversation back. But it was just the two of them most of the time, and she had to make the best of what she had.

When they got to the kitchen, Charlie sat him in his chair and set to making him some breakfast. She was moving a little faster than usual, but that was because she woke up late. She was supposed to be at the gym by eleven to meet the girls. Luckily, the gym wasn't too far away from MJ's daycare.

After they'd both eaten breakfast, Charlie got them dressed and ready to go. They were out the door within an hour. By the time she dropped him off and got to the gym, it was five minutes until eleven.

Mikayla was already inside, doing her stretches in the corner. The instructor was in front of the class, getting ready, and Charlie shot her a smile on her way over to Mikayla.

"Eme isn't here yet?" she asked, setting her yellow gym bag down beside Mikayla's.

"She's not coming. Something about locking in some entertainer for the luncheon."

"Oh, well, I guess that's important then," Charlie said and started stretching too. "I know for damn sure that I had to get out of that house. Mason has been damn near living in the office since the case with Jewel, and now there's that burglary turned homicide. Has he contacted you anymore about Jewel? He doesn't really talk to me about his cases."

"No, not yet. I'm working with Detective Janes on it too."

"Oh, yeah, the detective from the mortuary."

"Yeah. He's nice."

There was something about the way she said "nice," and Charlie caught it.

"What do you mean he's nice?"

"He's just been real helpful, that's all." Mikayla shrugged. "And we're going to go out for dinner."

"What!" Charlie exclaimed in a hushed tone so the other people in the gym wouldn't be all up in their business. "Girl, don't tell me that you're using Jewel's death to wax that monkey? Bitch, there is so much other dick in the world."

"You get on my damn nerves!" Mikayla said, laughing. "It's nothing like that. He's just nice, and I think I felt a spark when we were together. Nothing serious, but it was something, you know? I haven't felt *something* for anyone since Charles, and well, why not?"

"You don't have to explain shit to me, girl. I was just playing anyway. How is everything going with the funeral?"

"Good. Damian and I decided to just have a small gathering at the burial plot for anyone she knew to say their final goodbyes tomorrow. Damian is staying with me."

"What? The brother who you can't stand to be around for more than five minutes is staying with you?"

"Yeah. He's down on his luck and asked to stay with me for a little while," Mikayla said, shifting her gaze.

"And you said yes?"

"I mean, Jewel just died. And I don't know, I guess I just wanted to help. The past is the past, right?"

Charlie tried to study her girl, but Mikayla turned away. There was something strange about her whenever Damian was mentioned. Charlie didn't know the full extent of their childhood, but she guessed that it was very traumatizing. Mikayla rarely talked about it.

"Right," Charlie said, and just when she was about to change the subject, the door to the gym swung open.

A white man wearing a tucked-in button-up and a pair of jeans walked in and headed right over to Mikayla. When he was standing directly in front of her, he looked her up and down as if he were examining her.

"Mikayla King?" he asked.

"Yes, that's me," she said with a raised eyebrow.

He handed her a white envelope and she absentmindedly took it. "You've been served," he said, then walked out.

The rest of the people in the room were all staring at Mikayla. Some were whispering to each other, while others were pretending not to look, but Charlie could see them sneaking peeks in the mirror.

Mikayla looked stunned. She stared at the envelope in her hands for a few moments before she opened it. Her fingers moved slowly as she pulled the folded piece of paper out of it. When she unfolded it and started reading, Charlie could see Mikayla's face drop with every word.

"What is it?" Charlie asked.

"It's Charles. He's suing me for custody of the girls," Mikayla answered in a voice of disbelief. "Oh my God. He's going to try and take my girls."

"Come on, Kay Kay, let's get our stuff and go outside." She grabbed Mikayla's hand. "These motherfuckers can't mind their business," she said to the room while sneering at them.

They grabbed their things and headed outside. The air was brisk but not unbearable as they stood on the sidewalk. Mikayla looked as if she were about to cry, and Charlie felt sorry for her.

"He's not going to take your kids." She tried to soothe her.

"You don't know that. Charles is evil. He just wants to hurt me because I won't pull back on the divorce. The court date has been changed four times already, and now this!"

"He's just trying to buy himself time, that's all. Have you talked to him?"

"No. The girls have their own phones, and he gets them from school when it's his time with them. Who knows? He probably has been trying to contact me. I have him blocked everywhere but on my email."

"Then that's probably why he's doing this. He's probably just trying to get your attention. Give him a call."

"All he's going to try to do is meet me somewhere."

"And hell no, we're not having that."

"I'll just give him a call and see where it goes from there."

"That sounds good. Are you okay? Do you need anything?" Charlie asked.

"No, I'm all right. I'll just be happy when I can get off this roller coaster."

"I hear you, girl." Charlie gave Mikayla a quick hug. "Welp, since the workout vibe was completely killed, I'm gonna go 'head and go. I'm supposed to be hearing back from Shivelle today to see if our offer was accepted. I think I'ma go check out some décor. You want to come?"

"No, you go. Send me pictures of what you find. I'm going home so I can call this motherfucker."

They hugged one more time before parting ways.

As she drove away to the furniture store, Charlie thought about Mikayla. She might have been one of the strongest people Charlie knew. Even though she'd had a moment when she was abusing pills, Charlie understood. She tried to think back to a time Mikayla was really happy with Charles. There had never been huge red flags back then. Charlie just chalked her distance up to the fact that she had a man. Everybody knew that when your friends got into relationships you saw them less. It wasn't until Mikayla would pop up with mysterious bruises and then brush them off with some kind of excuse that Charlie started to sense something was wrong. Knowing what she knew about the situation now made her want to throw up. How could someone be so cruel to the person they vowed to love? And to continue to try to hurt them? Charlie knew Mikayla was fed up, but there was a light at the end of the tunnel, she just knew it.

On the way to the furniture department, Charlie had to pass one of Mason's favorite sandwich places. It was a family-owned spot called Wilson's. They served hot and cold sandwiches to your liking. The furniture store could wait. After all, Shivelle hadn't even called her yet.

Charlie pulled through the drive-through and ordered Mason's favorite, a Rueben melt with a side of onion rings. That time, she wasn't going to call her husband. She was just going to show up at the precinct.

When she got there, it was a chaotic sight to see. It must have been all hands on deck, because there were detectives bustling around left and right. It wasn't super loud, but there were many conversations going on at once. One of Mason's colleagues, Detective Hollins, spotted her when she came in and went over to her.

"Hey, Charlie," he said with a smile.

"Detective Hollins! It's good to see you. How's the wife?"

"She's good. On my ass about all this time I've had to spend at work, but you know how it is."

"Trust me, I do. But I understand. It must be like a hurricane in here with all this crime going on."

"Pshh, tell me about it," he said and ran his hand over his graying hair. "The murder of that woman went viral, and now 'torture' is trending online. It's ridiculous."

"Jewel? She was my best friend's mom," she said.

"Really? My condolences. I've never seen anything as monstrous as that. I don't know how her mother got herself into that mess, but from what they're saying, it wasn't good."

"What are they saying?"

"Word on the streets is that Jewel made some pretty bad decisions in the end and made enemies out of some bad people. I pray your friend isn't into anything like that."

"No, she's not," she said.

"Bringing Mason some lunch?" Detective Hollins asked, looking at the paper bag in her hand.

"Yes, I am. Is he in?" she asked, looking toward his office and noticing the blinds were closed.

"Yep, he's actually in his office with Detective Lawson. You want me to walk you back?"

"No, I think I can manage. Good seeing you."

She left him standing there and went back to her man's office. She hadn't met Detective Lawson yet, but it was a name she'd heard a few times around the house. She hoped she wasn't interrupting anything important, but that still didn't stop her from opening the door.

"Hi, honey. I was just bringing you some lun—" Charlie stopped mid-sentence.

Mason was sitting at his desk, smiling up at a woman who was standing a little too close for comfort. The woman was wearing a form-fitting pair of pants, and her white button-up blouse was tucked in and unbuttoned at the top. Her cleavage was inches away from Mason's face, and Charlie felt her hand tighten around the bag of food. The old Charlie wanted to hop out and beat the brakes off that bitch, but business-owner Charlie held her composure.

"Babe!" Mason said, looking shocked to see her standing there.

He cleared his throat, and Charlie saw a guilty look cross his face. He instantly moved away from the woman, but that didn't stop Charlie's cutting gaze. The woman smirked, and Charlie turned her attention to Mason before she slapped her.

"I came to bring you some lunch. I didn't know you were busy," Charlie said, looking distastefully at the woman.

"Detective Lawson was just showing me something on the computer," Mason said.

"With her titties all in your face?" Charlie asked bluntly.

"Excuse me?" Detective Lawson raised an eyebrow and rolled her neck.

"Get the fuck out of my man's office, and don't make me ask you twice." Charlie raised a lip at her.

Charlie had seen it as soon as she opened the office door, Detective Lawson's attraction to Mason. It was all in the way she looked at him. She had the puppy dog eyes of a high school freshman in love with a senior. Mason had never told her that Detective Lawson was a woman, and he should have, especially since they spent so much time together. *Especially* since she was gorgeous. Charlie didn't even know why a woman who looked like her was in law enforcement. She should have been half naked on somebody's magazine somewhere.

Detective Lawson looked at Mason as if to ask him what she should do, and that only made Charlie more irritated.

"Go on. I'll handle things here. We'll touch base on the case later," Mason told her.

"You got it, boss," Detective Lawson said and left the office.

Before she was gone, though, she gave Charlie a sly smile.

"What the fuck was that, Mason?" Charlie said, shutting the office door. "Huh?"

"What do you mean?" Mason asked. "I'm at work, working."

"With that bitch's boobs all in your face? And the door shut?"

"Baby, it's nothing like that," Mason said, getting up from his chair. "Detective Lawson was just in here helping me find a few documents. That's all."

"Why didn't I know she was a woman until now?"

"Because I knew you would act just like this," he said, walking toward her.

"No, it's because you want to be sneaky," Charlie said, stepping away from him. "That shit didn't just look right. And you've been away from home so much. Are you fucking her?"

"What?" Mason's eyes got big. "No! I'm not fucking her, Charlie. I promise you that. I don't want her or any other woman who isn't Charlie Dixon."

Charlie looked him in the eyes to try and find the truth in his words. She believed him, but Detective Lawson still made her very uneasy. She didn't like her.

"Well, you might not want her, but she sure wants you. It's written all over her face. I don't like it."

"Well, she is one of the lead detectives on this Tyrant case, so I have to work with her."

"Then tell that bitch to button up her shirt when she comes into work. Next thing you know, she might get mad and say you sexually assaulted her."

"I'll make sure I do that," Mason said and pulled her in for a kiss. When their lips disconnected, he took the bag from her hand. "Wilsons! Baby, you shouldn't have."

"Maybe I shouldn't have," Charlie said with a little disdain in her voice. "But I figured you'd be too swamped to be able to grab yourself something."

Mason took the food and went back to his desk. She thought he would say something else to her, but he just opened the bag and took his food out. He went back to scrolling on his computer like she wasn't standing right there.

He'd taken two bites of his sandwich before he noticed her still standing there. "I'm sorry, baby. Did you need anything else?" He looked at her like he was waiting for her to either say something or leave.

She was blown away. They had barely seen each other since he promised things would get better. It was like their lives paused for a moment, only for it to resume

with the regularly scheduled program. But still, she
thought that maybe they could talk for a second since
they hardly did at home.

"Nothing. I guess you have Detective Lawson here to
keep you company. You don't need me. I'm sure she'll be
right back in here when I leave."

"Charlie—" he started, but she didn't stay to hear
whatever he had to say.

She left his office, gritting her teeth. Her irritation
had turned to full-blown anger. There, she finally could
admit it. She was angry at Mason. He was neglecting
her. Yes, there were cases that needed to be solved, she
understood that, but they couldn't be more important
than his family falling apart. He hadn't even had the
decency to ask about how her day was or ask how Elegant
was coming along.

She walked all the way back to her car fighting the urge
to punch something the whole time. She was about to
scream into her steering wheel when the ringing of her
phone stopped her.

"Hello?" she snapped when she answered.

"Oh, was this a bad time?" Shivelle's voice came in from
the other end.

"Oh, I'm sorry. No," Charlie said, instantly changing
her tone. "What's going on?"

"What's going on is they accepted our offer. Elegant
officially has a physical address!" Shivelle told her excitedly.

"Well, after what just happened, believe me when I say
that's great news," Charlie told her. "More than great,
actually."

"Those designs you sent in were just lovely. I sent
them straight to the manufacturer. You'll have beautiful
dresses to fill the store in no time."

"I can't wait for it all to come together," Charlie said,
thinking about the inside of the store.

"I can't come in this upcoming weekend. My schedule is completely booked. But I can fly to Baltimore next weekend. Are you free?"

"My friend has a luncheon that day, but you are more than welcome to come with me to that."

"Perfect! I'll put it on my calendar. Mrs. Prichard can meet you whenever you're available to give you the keys."

"Would now work?"

"It should if you go right now. She's at the property."

"Okay, sounds good. And Shivelle?" Charlie asked before hanging up the phone.

"Yes, darling?"

"Thank you so much for everything. My entire life, I've never had anyone believe in me the way you do. I'm just a Baltimore girl, you know. Now my dreams are coming true."

"Don't thank me, dear. Your designs are going to shake the world. I may have been the first one to take notice, but believe me, your name is going to be known worldwide."

"Worldwide?"

"Think big, my dear Charlie. Kisses."

Shivelle disconnected the phone, leaving Charlie sitting alone in her car, still holding it to her ear. It took a second to remember that she was still in the parking lot of the precinct. She had so many emotions swirling around inside of her, and she didn't know which ones to bring to the forefront. She wanted to continue being angry at Mason, but that would take away from her happiness from her own accomplishments.

She put the phone away and contemplated going back in and giving Mason another piece of her mind, but then thought better of it. For the moment, she would choose happiness. If anything was being done in the dark, it would come to the light. And when it did, she would be right there waiting.

Chapter 11

Damian

The deep sleep he was in was interrupted when Damian had the sudden feeling he was being watched. His eyes shot open, and he blinked them a few times at the ceiling. It was the day of Jewel's burial, and he could swear he felt her presence, or the presence of somebody else. On the side of him, he heard the sound of snickering, and when he looked, he saw Zuri and Kai, his nieces, staring at him. He'd been staying with Mikayla for a couple days, but he hadn't really gotten to sit down to get to know them. He only knew who was who because Mikayla pointed them out in a picture downstairs. They were in their pajamas, and Kai, the younger one, had a yellow mug in her hands.

"We made you some hot chocolate," Kai said, holding the mug out.

Damian could see the steam radiating off of the hot liquid, and he also noticed that they'd put marshmallows on the top. Kai stared hopefully at him with her big, round doe eyes, and Damian felt like he had no choice. He sat up and put his back against his pillows before taking the mug.

"Kid, you're lucky you're cute. I don't like people interrupting my sleep," he told them. "You're also lucky that hot chocolate is one of my favorites. Thank you."

He thought that they would leave, but they stood there watching him like a hawk. The three of them were well

into their staredown when he realized they were waiting
for him to drink some. He placed the mug to his lips and
swallowed some of the hot chocolate.

"Are you really our uncle?" Zuri blurted.

"Yeah, I guess I am," he answered and put the mug on
the nightstand by the bed.

"You guess, or are you?" Zuri asked, placing her hands
on her hips.

"Yeah, or are you?" Kai mimicked her sister.

"I am."

"Then why haven't we ever met you?" Zuri asked.

"We never even heard about you before!" Kai exclaimed,
waving her hands.

Damian almost wanted to laugh at their theatrics. They
were cute, he had to give them that. Maybe when they were
older they would make great investigators, but right now,
they were in over their heads.

"That's something you'll have to speak to your mother
about," Damian told them, stretching his arms.

"You have some really big arms," Kai said, opening her
eyes big. "Are you a bodybuilder or something?"

"I've just lifted a lot of weights in my life," Damian told
her.

"In jail?" Kai asked.

"Kai!" Zuri gasped.

"What? I heard Mommy tell Auntie Charlie that he'd
been to jail before," Kai said, and Zuri tried to shush her.

"Nah, it's all right. Baby girl can speak her mind,"
Damian said. "I used to be a scrawny kid, but when I
went to jail, I bulked up like this."

"Maybe Mommy has pictures of you when you were a
kid like us!" Kai said excitedly.

"Yeah, maybe," Damian said doubtfully. He was sure
Mikayla had done everything in her power to remove
all of the memories from their childhood. Being in her

house, you would think she didn't have any family but her daughters and two friends. Their photos were the only ones she had up.

"Are you coming down to breakfast?" Zuri asked. "Mommy is making homemade waffles. She said they were your favorite when you guys were growing up."

"She remembered that?" he asked, slightly taken aback.

"Of course she did, silly. She's your sister!" Kai said, grabbing his hand and pulling on him. "Come on, let's go eat. Mommy makes the best bacon."

"With some fat on the pieces?" he asked her.

"Yes!" Kai's eyes lit up as she licked her lips.

"A'ight. You two go to the kitchen with your mom, and I'll be down in a second."

"Okay," Zuri said and took Kai's hand.

When they were gone and the guest bedroom door was shut again, Damian glanced down at the pillow on the other side of the bed. He was glad the girls hadn't gotten too close, because then they would have seen the handle of his Glock sticking out from under it. He grabbed the gun and put it in the nightstand before standing up and stretching his back. The flannel pajama pants and crisp white beater he'd worn to sleep still smelled like his favorite body spray. He stepped into his house shoes and left the room.

The aroma from the food cooking in the kitchen made his stomach grumble. He didn't know his sister could get down in the kitchen, but he would be the final judge of that. When he got to the entrance of the kitchen, he hung back before Mikayla could see him. He watched Mikayla pour waffle batter into the waffle iron. The girls stood behind her, watching their mother. Mikayla dipped her finger into the bowl of batter, quickly turned, and wipe the batter on Kai's nose. She then reached out and tickled Zuri. The girls giggled and ran away.

Damian smiled at the domestic scene playing out before him. He thought back to the things Jewel used to say about her when she would visit him in jail. Jewel said that she was selfish and didn't care about anybody but herself. But right then, Damian didn't see a selfish person. A sneeze snuck up on him and caught him by surprise, giving away his location.

The room got quiet, and Mikayla went back to cooking. Kai and Zuri went to sit down at the dining room table, and Kai motioned to the empty seat between them.

"Come sit with us, Uncle Damian," she said.

He glanced at Mikayla before he did anything, and she nodded her head.

"I'll bring your plate to you," she said. "You want a waffle, eggs, bacon, and some fruit?"

"Shit, sounds good to me," he said before he could catch himself.

Zuri gasped, but Kai giggled. Mikayla glared at him and looked as if she wanted to say something. She didn't, though. She just went back to fixing their plates.

Damian went and sat between the girls. Zuri poured him a tall glass of orange juice from the pitcher in the center of the table, and Kai handed him a napkin.

"You two always this polite?"

"Mommy says ladies are always this polite."

"It wasn't too polite of you to bust in my room like the police this morning and ask me a million questions."

"Hey! We did not bust in there like the police!" Kai exclaimed. "The police don't have hot chocolate."

Damian chuckled. Zuri put him a lot in the mind of Mikayla, but Kai reminded him of himself. Before his childhood was stolen from him, that is.

He sipped his orange juice as Mikayla brought them their plates and sat down herself. Once Damian got one whiff of his food, he knew it wasn't going to be a murder scene on his plate. Kai watched with her mouth open as he scarfed down his food.

"Girl, eat your own food," Zuri told her. "It's so rude to just stare."

"It's so rude to just stare," Kai mocked her in a baby voice.

"Mom!"

"Girls, stop it," Mikayla said. "It's too early, and it's enough that you're out of school today as it is."

Ding! Dong!

Damian could tell by the perplexed look on Mikayla's face that she hadn't been expecting company. That and the fact that she was still in her pajamas and robe. She excused herself and went to see who was at the door.

Damian continued to eat his food with the girls, but he kept his ears open. He couldn't make out what was being said, but he could have sworn he heard distress in Mikayla's voice.

"You two stay here and finish your breakfast. I'll be right back," he said, but Kai and Zuri were both too focused on their phones. Damian shook his head. When he first got out of jail, it had been a big adjustment for him. They'd had access to computers inside, but to basically have one in the palm of your hand was still crazy to him.

He left the dining room to see who was at the door. Bone had said he would be watching, and Damian wanted to make sure it wasn't someone that he'd sent. However, it wasn't. It was Charles, Mikayla's husband. Well, soon-to-be ex-husband. A while back, Damien had heard Mikayla's friends shouting something about him putting his hands on Mikayla, but at that time, Damian had a lot of malice in his heart, so he didn't really care. Now, he didn't know what he felt as he watched Charles look smugly at Mikayla.

"Why are you doing this?" Mikayla was saying. "I never ever said that I would stop you from seeing the girls. Now you're trying to *take* them from me?"

"This is about the well-being of the girls," Charles said. "You're too busy for them. Zuri told me that they barely see you anymore since you started doing whatever you think you're doing."

"I'm an advocate for domestic violence, and I now get paid to speak my mind, so yes, I am a little more busy than I was when I was your doormat. But that has nothing to do with my capability to parent!" Mikayla shot back.

"I think it does," Charles said. "The girls aren't happy. They've told the therapist that many times."

"Therapist?"

"Oh, they didn't tell you?" he asked her with a sickening smile. "During their time with me, the girls have been seeing a therapist, one of the best in the city. And they have told her some pretty interesting things. Like how you forgot to pick them up from school more than once and you had to have one of your friends grab them."

"I didn't forget them. I would never forget them! Sometimes I run late. Everybody does. But thankfully, I have friends to have my back," she said, glaring at him.

"They also said that they saw a bottle of pills in your bathroom," Charles said, and Mikayla's eyes widened. "Why even make me take you to court? Just give me my girls."

"You don't want them," Mikayla said in a shaky voice. "You just don't want me to have them. You're only doing this because I don't want to be with you."

"If I can't have you . . ." Charles let his voice trail and tried to step around her. "I think I'm going to go say hello to my girls."

"No! You're not! I want you out of my house!" she said through clenched teeth.

She tried to stop him, but he was already past her. Before he could get past the front hallway, however, Damian stepped out of the shadows. Charles stopped in his tracks, looking dumbfounded at Damian's big build.

"My sister said she wants you out of her house," Damian said, giving Charles an icy stare. "Mikayla, go back in there with Kai and Zuri so they don't get curious. It's almost time for them to start getting ready, isn't it?"

Mikayla hesitated, but seeing that Damian wasn't going to let Charles pass, she went back to the dining room. Charles sized Damian up, and the dumbfounded look on his face turned into a sly smile.

"I met you back at the hospital," he said. "You're Damian, right?"

"That's right."

"Yeah, yeah." Charles wagged his finger. "I did some digging on you."

"Did you now?"

"Yeah, I did. Found out some pretty interesting things, too."

"I bet you did. Too bad I already know everything about my life," Damian said.

"You know what I think? I think that it was somebody else who pulled that trigger."

"It's a good thing you aren't getting paid for what you think."

"Well, what would you say if I told you I *know* somebody else pulled the trigger?"

"I did the time for that already."

"Time that should have been somebody else's," Charles hinted and reached in his pocket for a business card. "I know you're on hard times, otherwise you wouldn't be staying with somebody you and I both know you hate. I think we can help each other out. Call me."

He placed the card on the table and left. When Damian heard the door shut completely, he picked up the card and stared at it. Damian felt that Charles might have really known something, and the only way to find out would be to call. But it would have to be later, after he buried his mother.

Damian rode with Mikayla and the girls to the grave site. The two of them didn't say anything on the drive about what had happened at breakfast, but there was definitely some tension in the air. He kept seeing her glance over at him out of his side view, but she never said anything. When they got there, the girls were the first ones out of the car. Damian was surprised that Mikayla had brought them along, since she and Jewel didn't get along. Maybe she thought that because they were older kids, it would be all right.

When he got out, he felt someone grab his hand, and when he looked down, he saw Kai smiling up at him. He couldn't resist smiling back. They walked to where Jewel's casket was already positioned over her plot, and she let go of his hand. He stood in front of the casket and just stared at the brown wood. He hadn't seen her body before they put her inside, but Mikayla told him that she looked pretty bad.

"Mikayla!" a voice yelled.

They all looked down by where they'd parked and saw two women and a man walking toward them. Damian recognized the two women as Mikayla's friends, but he didn't know the man.

"Charlie! Emerson! I thought I told you that you didn't have to come." Mikayla gave them both hugs when they reached her.

"We know, but we came anyway. Eme wanted to stop and grab you a bottle of wine," Charlie said with a grin.

"That would have been great, actually," Mikayla told her and then motioned her hands toward Damian. "I don't think any of you have properly met each other. You guys, this is my brother, Damian. He's been staying with me until we bury Jewel. Damian, this is Charlie, Emerson, and Mason."

"Nice to meet you, man," Mason said, shaking his hand. "I'm sorry for your loss. I'm actually a lead detective on the case, so if you find out anything in regards to what happened, let me know."

Damian nodded his response. Mason was the only one out of the three who spoke. The other two just kind of looked at him distastefully, but Damian didn't care. A few more people nobody knew came to pay their last respects to Jewel. He turned back to face the casket and left Mikayla to fellowship with her loved ones and the newcomers.

It was a strange feeling, knowing that he had to say goodbye before he was ready. He had been moving around by himself for the past couple of years, but it wasn't until then that he truly felt alone. There was no one left in the world that he could call on and who he would hear "I love you" from. The ache in his chest came on suddenly as the reality of the situation hit him. He would never see her again. He'd lost so many years with her and only had gotten two back. Life was cruel that way.

What were you doing here, Mama? he thought to himself. *And whatever it was, why didn't you tell me about it? I could have protected you, but now you're dead.*

When she was lowered into the ground, everyone there threw a rose on her casket, and Damian said a prayer. He blinked away the tears, hearing Jewel's voice in his head.

Now, you know you don't have to cry, baby.
Everything is all right now.

That was what she had said when he walked through
the prison doors a free man. He'd been so overwhelmed
that he shed a few tears in front of her. She caught them
all and comforted him. Now, since she wasn't there to
catch his tears, he just refused to let them fall.

He'd been thinking about the diamond Jewel stole
and how he was going to recover it. She was a wild card,
but one thing about her was that she kept up with the
things she cared about. He couldn't see her misplacing
something as valuable as a million-dollar diamond. No.
She had put it up somewhere, and it was up to him to
figure out where.

He looked back at the people he didn't recognize and
found himself wondering if they'd seen her before she
passed. One of them specifically caught his attention. She
had come alone and was standing away from everyone
else, like him. She looked to be about Jewel's age and
wore a long black coat over her black dress. She had
smooth, peanut-butter skin, and her long hair was pulled
back in a braided ponytail.

Damian stepped back and approached the lady. Her
eyes were still on the casket, but she'd felt him come up
to her. He knew, because she gently and quickly touched
his hand.

"You're her youngest, Damian," she stated.

"That's right. Who are you, and how did you know my
mother?"

"I'm Oddette, but all of my friends call me Oddie.
Jewel called me that. You can too. We met at the job we
were working at. A cleaning job in Indiana. Jewel had
just started working there maybe a year ago. It wasn't a
regular cleaning job, though."

"How so?" Damian's interest was piqued.

"Our job was to clean houses that other cleaning services wouldn't be able to . . . handle, I guess you can say," she said, turning to face him and looking him dead in the eye. "Sometimes blood would be on the kitchen floor, and we would clean it up and ask no questions."

"Y'all cleaned the houses of criminals?" Damian asked, putting two and two together.

"Eh. None of them have been convicted yet." Oddie shrugged. "We got paid well for it."

"Clearly not well enough if we were here to—" He stopped midsentence.

He'd almost told her they were there to blackmail his sister. Oddie looked back to where Mikayla was, and then back to Damian. She gave him a knowing look with a sad smile.

"I know why you were here, but that's not really why you were *here*," she told him. "Jewel knew the only way you'd come back to Baltimore was if some money was involved. So she said what she had to say to get you here, but she never planned to extort that girl more than she already had."

"Why are you telling me this?"

"Because you need to know the reason your mother is dead," she said forcefully but in a hushed tone. She had Damian's full attention. "The last person we worked for, we never saw or met. Everything was fine, until one day, Jewel found a ring and snuck it into her pocket. She told me that it had fallen into a vent and that nobody would miss it, but I think she took it right from the master bedroom. I don't think she thought anything of it, since we hadn't had any bloody encounters in that house. But she was wrong. She'd stolen from someone very dangerous, and he noticed."

"Tyrant," Damian said.

"Yeah," she said, surprised. "How do know that?"

"Because one of his henchman paid me a visit a few days ago. Told me that if I don't find the diamond or pay what it's worth, then they're gonna—"

"Kill you," Oddie finished for him.

"And my son," Damian added.

"A son? Jewel never mentioned a grandson."

"Because she didn't know about him," Damian said in a pained voice, and Oddie gave him a sympathetic stare. "Why did she do it?"

"For you, and for her." Oddie nodded her head backward toward Mikayla. "She sometimes talked about all that she would do different as a mother. When she found out how much the diamond was worth, I think she looked at it as a second chance to make old wrongs right.

"She quit right after and moved here when we found out who she had stolen from. A man came to visit me last month and told me that he was the Bone Collector. Said that they have Jewel on camera taking something very valuable, and if I knew what's best for me, then I would tell him where she ran off to. But I didn't know where she was, and I told him that. I guess he believed me, because I'm still breathing. l didn't find out that she was in Baltimore until I found out she was dead. But . . ."

"But what?"

"She called me a little while after that incident and told me that she felt like someone was following her, and that if anything ever happened to her, to tell her son to check the vent in the bathroom of her apartment."

"The vent in the bathroom of her apartment?" Damian repeated to be clear.

"That's what she said, and it was the last thing she ever said to me. I'll remember it for the rest of my life," Oddie said and placed a hand on his shoulder.

Damian looked in her eyes to see if she was telling the truth. "Why haven't you gone to check to see what was in the vent?"

"Remember, I cleaned this person's home. I know how vicious he can be. I want no part of any of this," she said. "Good luck to you. And be careful."

With that, she walked away and didn't stop to speak to anyone else.

Mikayla wasn't the only one giving Oddie and Damian curious eyes. Mason was too. Damian ignored them and headed back to the car. The sooner he got back to his own vehicle the sooner he would be able to get to her apartment.

Chapter 12

Mason

After attending the burial of Mikayla's mother, Mason took Charlie home to relieve MJ's babysitter. When he was satisfied that Charlie and MJ were settled, he went to work. On the way there, he couldn't stop thinking about Damian and the older woman. There was something about that whole exchange that wasn't sitting right with Mason. He wished he'd been close enough to hear their conversation. He just knew they were talking about details surrounding Jewel's murder, but he had no proof.

There hadn't been any more big breaks in the case since Mason found the symbol, but for some reason he felt that he would find some answers if he went back to her apartment. Without thinking, Mason switched the direction he was going. Instead of driving to the precinct, he went to Jewel's place.

When he reached the small complex, he parked and took in his surroundings before getting out. Nothing seemed out of the ordinary, but he did take notice of a Cadillac parked at the curb directly in front of Jewel's building. It seemed out of place to Mason. He did one more look around the area before getting out of his car. He checked to make sure the gun on his hip was secure when he stepped out of the car.

Upon reaching Jewel's apartment, he saw the yellow tape had been ripped apart and the door was slightly ajar.

He rested his hand on his firearm as he stepped to the door. He heard shuffling coming from inside. Somebody was there. Could it be Tyrant making sure there were no loose ends? He quietly entered the apartment and drew his gun for his safety.

The noise was coming from the kitchen, and when Mason got there he saw a tall man placing something on top of the refrigerator. He aimed his gun at the man's back.

"Freeze!" he said loudly. "Turn around and face me with your hands up. Slow!"

The man followed instructions, and when he was turned completely around, Mason relaxed his trigger finger and let out a relieved breath. "Damian," he said and lowered his gun. "I thought you were someone else. What are you doing here?"

"The landlord just told me that Mama was paid up to the end of the month, and technically all of this stuff is mine now," Damian said, gesturing to the chaotic mess. "Whoever did it really did a number on this place. They even cut the couches and mattress open."

"Whatever they were after must have been important," Mason said and decided he would tempt the pot to see if Damian knew anything. "Does the name Tyrant ring a bell to you?"

The moment Mason said the name, he saw a look of recognition flicker across Damian's face. Damian tried to mask it, but it was too late. Mason could see he knew something.

"What do you know?" Mason pressed. "If you have any clue of what happened to your mother, tell me. I can help you. We both want the same thing."

"Yeah, and what's that?"

"To put the son of a bitch who did this to Jewel away."

"See, that's where you're wrong, Mr. Detective. I don't want shit but to put this behind me. Matter of fact, you're questioning me, but what are *you* even doing here?"

"I thought I would come and make sure we didn't miss anything, and then I found you here. Do you know something, Damian? Who was that you were talking to at the funeral?"

"I didn't know her. She was Mama's friend. Said they met recently on a job in Indiana. I didn't even know Mama had moved to Indiana."

"Is that all she said?" Mason asked, and Damian sighed big.

"You can't just leave the way you came in, man?"

"No, and you shouldn't want me to if you have information that could help us both."

"A'ight. She said her and Mama did some house cleaning. On a job, Jewel swiped a diamond that belonged to Tyrant."

"A diamond? He did all of this for one measly diamond?"

"A diamond worth one million dollars," Damian corrected. "And yeah, I guess he did. I mean, Mama is in the dirt, ain't she?"

"I'm sorry. I didn't mean to be insensitive, but wow," Mason said, wrapping his head around what Damian had just said. "This motherfucka Tyrant really doesn't play about his debts, does he?"

"No, he really doesn't," Damian said absentmindedly, and Mason raised a brow.

"What does that mean?"

"Huh? Oh, nothing, man," he said and averted his eyes from Mason's. "I just mean that all of this is so crazy. It feels like I just got out of prison. I thought I would be able to start over, but instead it feels like I'm frozen in place. Stuck in a bad reality. But I don't know anything else, and if you don't mind, I have a lot of cleaning to do, as you can see. You know where the door is."

"A'ight, you got it," Mason said, nodding his head. "But if anything jogs your memory, you know how to get a hold of me."

Mason started to leave, but he stopped and turned back to Damian.

"Something else?" Damian asked with a hint of annoyance.

"Yeah, one more thing. Do you know if the diamond ever turned up?"

"No." Damian shook his head. "I don't know if it did or not."

"Yeah, well, hopefully Tyrant just calls it even since Jewel is dead. I hope he doesn't pass her debt onto someone else."

Mason left without another word. He felt that Damian wanted to say more than what he was laying on, but he didn't press the fact any more than he already had.

Mason got back in his car. He barely even remembered the ride to the precinct because he was replaying the conversation with Damian for any clues he might have missed. This case was becoming more complicated the more information he gathered.

When he got back to the precinct, he sat down in front of the evidence wall in his office. In the center was a photo of a male silhouette with a question mark on it that represented Tyrant.

Mason jotted down all of the things Damian had just told him and placed them on the wall so that he could try to connect the dots. Why had Jewel chosen Baltimore to run to? Anyone with access to a computer could find out Jewel's only daughter resided there. It would have been one of the first places anybody would check. Also, Mikayla hadn't had any assets, nor were there any bank accounts in her name. If she had sold the diamond, there were so many places she could have hidden the money, and the only two people he could think of who could know the location of it were Jewel's two children. But that was only if she sold it.

Mason sighed, feeling like he had yet another cold case on his hands.

"Who is Tyrant?" he said out loud to himself.

Knock! Knock!

He turned his head to the office door. Nobody opened his door before he told them it was okay to open it but Charlie. He just knew she would be standing there, and he almost got excited, but he saw that it was just Detective Lawson.

"Hey, I'm sorry for barging in," she said and held up some paperwork in her hands. "I came by earlier and knocked, but you weren't here."

"I'm sorry, Lawson," Mason said, wiping his hands down the front of his face. "I'm just trying to work this case out."

"Well, I don't want to be the bearer of bad news, but we might have to pull the plug on the investigation altogether," Lawson said, shutting his door before she went and dropped the papers on his desk. "The Chief Superintendent went over the file you just sent in."

"And he wants to pull the plug on it?" Mason asked incredulously. "I know it's early, but if he just gives us some more time, I'm confident that we are on the right track to finding out who Tyrant is. We just need more time."

"He said that there isn't enough evidence to pursue."

"The symbols match up from two similar crime scenes. He *can't* think that they are just a coincidence."

"It's not that. He just thinks that going after this Tyrant character is the wrong move right now," Lawson said.

"And what do you think?" Mason asked.

"I think that I would really like to figure out what happened to Jewel Birmingham. But I also don't want to lose my job by disobeying orders to take a missing swing," she told him honestly. She walked over to him and placed her hand on his shoulder. "The noise from all of this is almost completely quiet. And there are other cases with higher priority. I'm sorry, Mason."

"Damnit!" He hit the arm of his chair.

"Better five solved cases out of ten than no solved cases because you're chasing one."

He hated to admit that she was right, but she was. He didn't want her to be, though. But if his boss was telling him to drop it, then he had no other choice. He might have fought harder if he had more to go on, but he was chasing a ghost.

He glanced at the evidence board one more time before letting out a small groan. It wasn't until he felt Lawson's thumb move that he remembered her hand was on his shoulder. He looked from her hand to her face, thinking she would get the point and move it, but she didn't. He cleared his throat, but she still didn't move her hand.

"Well, besides busting my balls and telling me to stop working a case I've been spending all my time on, was there anything else you wanted, Lawson?"

"Yes, actually there is," she said.

Without warning, Lawson straddled him in his chair. Her lips were on his before he could fully comprehend what was happening. The hand that had been on his shoulder was now behind his neck, mushing his face into hers, making it impossible to pull away. When she broke the kiss, she tried to unbutton his shirt, but he grabbed her hands.

"Lawson, what the hell are you doing?" he asked in a horrified tone.

"Don't act like you don't want it, Mason. I see the way you smile at me. You want me. I know you do."

"Smile at you? I smile at everybody!" Mason said and pushed her off his lap. "Now, Lawson, I don't know what's come over you, but you have to know that what you just did was completely inappropriate."

"Inappropriate?" she asked with a laugh. "Mason, it's okay. We're two consenting adults, and I know how to keep a secret. You don't have to worry about anybody who works here finding out about us."

She tried to make a move on him again, but Mason stopped her.

"Us? There is no *us*, Lawson. Look, you're a good-looking woman, and any man would be happy to have you. Any *single* man."

"Technically, you are single." Lawson pouted. "You aren't married."

"But I am in a relationship. You know this. You've met Charlie!"

"I met the woman you put a baby in but haven't made your wife. There is a difference. In my eyes, you don't have a ring, so you're single."

Mason didn't have a rebuttal right away. Was that really how women thought? Technically, it was true. Legally being boyfriend and girlfriend held no bounds, but still, a level of respect should come with that from all sides. Of course Mason wanted to marry Charlie. However, he didn't know what was holding him back from popping the question. It wasn't until then that he'd ever even asked himself that. Was it because he already had one failed marriage under his belt? Had he gotten comfortable with how things were? He didn't know the answer to either one of those questions, and that was a problem. Lawson being in front of him the way she was right then proved that.

"Detective Lawson," he started, "as your boss, I'm going to tell you to never approach me like this again. It's unprofessional, and if it ever happens again, I will relieve you of all duties. Do you understand me?"

Detective Lawson stood there looking dumbfounded that he had rejected her. Her mouth opened and closed repeatedly, and she stuttered over her words. When she finally put herself together again, she stood up straight and held her head high.

"I understand, Mason."

"Call me Detective Lieutenant Dale," Mason corrected. "You can leave, and hopefully you really think about your actions. I'll be documenting this just in case you try and spin what happened for your benefit, and also remember that I do have a camera in this office."

If Lawson had been thinking about filing sexual harassment charges against Mason because he rejected her, those plans were quickly spoiled. Mason wasn't going to play those kinds of games with her or anyone else. He took his job seriously, and he wasn't willing to jeopardize it or his relationship for a piece of pussy.

Lawson tucked her tail and hightailed it to the door.

"Lawson," Mason called out before she left. "Just a little advice for the next time you're interested in a guy, a hopefully single guy. A man who has reached a certain height of respect and maturity doesn't really like for a woman to throw herself at him. It's in a man's nature to hunt, and we don't like anything that comes too easy. Practice a little restraint. I'm sure Prince Charming will come sooner than later."

For a moment, she stared blankly at him. But when his words settled in, she smiled faintly. She didn't say anything else to him, and instead left quietly. When she was gone, Mason let out a loud breath and set out to take down his evidence board.

Chapter 13

Emerson

The Empowering With Love Luncheon came faster than Emerson thought it would. The venue they booked was big enough to host one thousand people, and every ticket had been purchased. Almost every attendee had also purchased a meal voucher and a meet and greet package. Emerson had been able to use her influence to snag Esha, an up and coming Baltimore singer, and the buzz from that alone was enough to carry the luncheon. There were a few public speakers booked as well, and Emerson was excited for the information they had to give. She hoped the women walked away feeling bossy and like they could do anything.

In the days leading up to the event, Emerson wrestled with the idea of asking Jacob to attend with her. On one hand, it would give the impression of a power couple, but on the other hand, she didn't want to encourage Jacob and give him the false impression that she was more committed than she was. Her first priority was to her business. In the end, she decided Jacob could be her date.

They were sitting at dinner when she asked him. They had just ordered their meals, and the waiter had opened a bottle of wine.

Emerson took a sip and said, "I was thinking you might want to come to my luncheon."

Jacob smiled. "There's nothing else I'd want to do than to watch my woman run the show and see her in her element." He reached for her hand.

She smiled, hiding the fact she was second guessing her invitation.

Jacob squeezed her hand. "I can't wait until we live in the same house and get ready for these events together."

Now he was jumping the gun and talking about living together. Emerson didn't want Jacob to feel like she was distancing herself from him since he said the *L* word, but maybe that was what she needed to do. He claimed he didn't want to rush her, but it was obvious he was ready to speed things along. Emerson honestly didn't know if she was ready for all that. Not to mention Cali was still in the picture. She didn't want to break her heart and have another Macy on her hands. It was too much. Emerson just wanted to enjoy the luncheon that she'd worked so hard to put together.

At the event, Cecil Tilson, a former CNN newscaster, was on stage speaking, but Emerson and her guests were more focused on each other. They were seated at a table in the front of the ballroom and over to the side. It was the perfect vantage point to see the entire ballroom, the stage, and to have their own conversation without anyone hearing. Mikayla had already met Jacob by accident, but of course, Charlie dragged it out.

"It's so good to *finally* meet the man that's been putting a smile on our friend's face," she said, placing a hand over her heart. "I thought your name was Casper at first."

"Charlie," Mikayla said and rolled her eyes.

"What? I'm just saying. I can't believe you two have been dating for so long and nobody knew. But Eme has always been the best out of all of us about being low key."

"She definitely has some mystery about her," Jacob chimed in, smiling at Emerson. He gave her a pair of eyes that said he wished he could eat her up right then and there. It made Emerson uncomfortable, and she hoped that no one else caught the look.

Jacob continued, "Baby, if I haven't told you already, you look stunning in that dress. The blue is so light, it's almost white."

"Thank you, baby," Emerson said, blushing. "Charlie designed it. She's gifted with her hands."

"Oh, that's right. Emerson said you were opening a store soon. How is that coming?"

"Great! I actually just closed on a location thanks to my investor," Charlie answered, beaming as she spoke.

"That's great. I'm all for black business. The more the merrier. When do you plan to be open for business?"

"In a little over a month. As long as my inventory comes in on time."

"Where is Shivelle?" Emerson asked. "I thought you said she was going to be here today."

"She's here, but baby partied too hard last night," Charlie said, giving her a look. "We went out for drinks, and she went in on the shots. We're supposed to be meeting up later. I just hope everything turns out the way I see it in my head."

"And it will. Positive thoughts only," Emerson told her and then turned to Mikayla, who was sitting next to Charlie. "You all right? I feel like I haven't spoken to you since Jewel was buried."

It was true. After her mother was put in the ground, Mikayla had been a little withdrawn. It wasn't something Emerson was used to anymore, since she'd left Charles. For the past two years, Emerson had watched Mikayla come completely out of her shell. Now it was like she was trying to inch back inside. Emerson had even asked Mikayla to speak at the luncheon, but she turned down the offer. Charlie had said something about Charles serving her with papers while they were at the gym, but Emerson hadn't heard any more about it. She just hoped everything was okay.

"I'm good. Just dealing with a few things, but nothing I can't manage," Mikayla said with a reassuring smile.

"Is Damian still staying with you?"

"No He left after the burial. I haven't heard from him."

"Well, I'm sure you have some peace of mind. You don't have to worry about your shit walking out the door when you aren't there."

"Charlie!" Emerson said, cutting her eyes at her.

"Don't say my name like that. We all know that nigga looks sketchy as fuck. Kay Kay might have walked in and all her good silverware was gone. Wait—" Charlie turned to Mikayla. "Did the nigga take your good China?"

"I'm so sorry." Emerson turned to apologize to Jacob, who was cracking up laughing.

Emerson's co-host, Jamar Brown, approached the table and touched her shoulder. She glanced up and smiled at him. He was a handsome, openly gay man and could outdress everyone she knew. Jamar also had his own large following for his brand, and it was the first event he and Emerson had done together. He thought his presence at a Women's Empowerment event would speak volumes for the LGBT community. Emerson agreed. The check he came with was also a big reason she teamed up with him. He was matching her ten thousand dollars to donate to She Is Success, a trade school program for young women right out of high school. They were supposed to be making an announcement about it during the luncheon.

"Jamar!" Emerson gushed and checked the golden linked watch on her wrist. "Is it time to make the announcement already?"

"No, not yet. After Cecil, Esha is up next, singing her new song."

"Ooooh, Cherry Sunday? I love that song," Charlie gushed. "It's about a girl asking why the man she loves ignores her the way we do a cherry on an ice cream sundae. It's such a beautiful play on words. For her to be so young, she's deep, okay?"

"I think someone has a fan over here," Mikayla joked, and Charlie pretended to pinch her.

"I just wanted to say that this turned out to be such a wonderful event," Jamar said, taking Emerson's hand in his. "I'm so sorry I wasn't involved with much of the planning, but you did the damn thing, honey."

"Look, as long as your check clears, we are all good." Emerson laughed.

"Oh, trust me. It's going to clear. And I'll be glad to do business with you again."

He kept talking, but something behind him had taken hold of Emerson's attention. A woman had just walked through the doors and was heading right for their table. As she got closer, Emerson realized it was Cali. She was dressed up in a long, form-fitting emerald green dress with her hair pulled back, looking gorgeous as usual. But that didn't matter at the moment. Emerson felt a pit in her stomach, wondering why Cali was there. She hadn't been invited specifically because Jacob was going to be there.

When she got to the table, she gave Emerson a sneaky smile before waving her fingers at everyone else. Emerson opened her mouth to ask her what she was doing there, but Jacob surprisingly beat her to the punch.

"Late as usual," he said to Cali and stood up to kiss her on the cheek.

"I might have had a minor wardrobe malfunction," Cali said sweetly.

"It's all right. You're here now," Jacob told her. He took her hand and turned to Emerson. "I'm sorry, baby. I forgot to tell you. I invited someone to join us today. I want you to meet my niece, Cali."

Chapter 14

Charlie

Kicking her shoes off when she walked in, Charlie was surprised to see Mason on the living room couch. He put his finger to his lips before she could speak and pointed to the other couch. MJ was lying there, sound asleep under his favorite blue blanket. Mason quietly stood up and went to where she was standing to help her take off her coat, but she shook her head.

"I got it," she told him.

Charlie wasn't in the mood to pretend things were good between them. He hadn't even said anything about the long-sleeved, off-the-shoulder sweater dress she designed and made for herself. It stopped just over her knees, and the sock booties on her feet made her sit up in all the right places. She was sure that when she walked down the stairs before she left, he would be drooling all over her. But Mason had been so engrossed in his work folder that he probably didn't even see her. Or maybe he didn't care.

She took off her coat and went upstairs without saying a word to him. All that was on her mind was changing into something more comfortable and lying down. After those bottomless mimosas, a nap sounded like a good idea.

It was only four o'clock, but Charlie still slid into her nightgown before getting into the bed. She had just snuggled under the covers and closed her eyes when she felt a hand shake her back gently.

"Hey, baby. MJ is moving like he's about to wake up," he said. "Do you think you can get him so I can get some work done?"

Charlie opened one eye to turn and look at him. He was standing there with that black leather folder in his hands, and all she wanted to do was take it and throw it. It was all he seemed to care about.

"After I take a nap," she said and rolled over.

"Baby, I really need to get back to work. I've been on Dad duty since you left this morning. I haven't been able to do a thing."

That was it. Charlie had had it. She sat up in the bed and glared at him.

"I'm on Mommy duty every day, and the only help you give me is to come play with him for a little bit and then give him back to me," she said with attitude dripping off every word. "I had to enroll him in daycare just so I can get things done, and you didn't even want me to do *that*."

"Because I thought we agreed we would keep him home until he's three."

"No, *you* agreed that we could keep him home until he's three. But now, things are different. I'm starting a business, Mason," Charlie told him in an exasperated voice. "And you don't even seem to care."

"Charlie, excuse me if I think that if all you're doing is going to the fabric store, you can have your son. I actually have to work. I'm sorry if me saving lives is more important than some hobby of yours right now. But I promise—"

"Hobby?" she scoffed. "Did you just call what I'm doing a hobby?"

"Charlie." Mason sighed. "I'm just stating facts. If it isn't producing income, then it's a hobby."

She looked at him like he had just slapped her in the face. Had he really not noticed all of her hard work? Did he really think that she was in their fourth bedroom, which was filled with sewing materials, making things just for the fun of it? What made it so bad was that she'd told him how she wanted to be a fashion designer one day. She couldn't even put the words together to say to him. She wanted to tell him how she had a millionaire investing in her business. She wanted to tell him that she had just closed on a location. She wanted to tell him how she had gowns that *she* designed being imported from Paris, but she didn't. Instead, she lay back down with her back to him.

"Are you going to get him, or not?"

"I just said I wanted to take a nap," she told him, closing her eyes again. "I would tell you to hire a babysitter, but you might start fucking her too."

She thought he would have something to say back to that, but he didn't. She heard him groan behind her and shuffle back out of the room.

When Charlie woke up, she got dressed and left with MJ. Mason didn't even try to talk to her. He had a look of longing in his eyes, but he just let her go. She was glad, because she didn't want to argue anymore that day. Did she really think deep down that Mason would cheat on her? No. But it still bothered her that another woman was getting any of his attention when she wasn't getting any.

She didn't want to wallow in her self-pity when she was taking MJ to her store for the first time. She and Shivelle had planned on meeting there that evening to look at the walls to see what kinds of shelves they would need to order. Shivelle wanted to get metal shelves, but Charlie wanted glass.

When she got there, Charlie was surprised to see the lights on already. Shivelle was there, walking around with a notebook and jotting things down. Charlie sat MJ down on the floor with his blanket and tablet before approaching her.

"I see you're among the land of the living again," Charlie joked. "And styling at that." She snapped her fingers at Shivelle's outfit. She was wearing a peach blazer dress and had her hair in a braided bun at the top of her head. Shivelle might have been ten years Charlie's senior, but she was the epitome of "black don't crack." If she didn't tell you, you would never know her age.

"Oh, you better stop it. I already got you the store. You don't have to sucker up to me anymore," Shivelle said, swatting her hand playfully. She then held up the notebook in her other hand and pointed at something she'd scribbled. "So, now that I'm inside here again, I think you're right."

"About what?"

"The shelves. I think the glass would give Elegant a look of elegance."

"Yes!" Charlie cheered. "I knew you would see my vision. And since we're doing glass shelves, I'm thinking we should keep the theme with the racks. We also need to get some blush-colored cocktail ottomans to go right there. Oh! And two blush sofas back there by the dressing room."

Charlie continued to ramble off all the things she saw in her head when she imagined the finished product of her store. She knew everything she wanted and where everything would go.

She was so busy talking that she didn't even notice the wonderous look that Shivelle was giving her.

"What?" she asked when she finally stopped to take a breath.

"You just have it all mapped out, I see. You don't need my help at all," Shivelle said with a small smile.

"Oh." Charlie's face dropped when she realized she hadn't stopped to ask for her investor's input. "I'm sorry. I just got so carried away. I haven't even asked what you think would be a good setup in here."

"Don't apologize," Shivelle said, shutting her notebook. "What you just described sounds lovely. In fact, I'm so pleased that you have your shit together. I'm so used to being hands on when it comes to taking on new tasks, but this? This is refreshing. And the best part is that you believe in Elegant, so I do too. I think this time I will just let this investment of mine blossom."

"It feels good to hear *somebody* say they believe in me," Charlie told her. "My boyfriend thinks that all of this is still a hobby."

"Charlie, you mean to tell me that you still haven't told that man about all of your good news?" Shivelle was shocked. "How do you hide all of this when you live in the same house?"

"I don't hide anything, and I'd be more adamant to talk about it if his face wasn't always buried in his work folder. Girl, you should have seen me when I left for the luncheon! I wore the Delon dress I designed. Ass looking scrumptious, thighs were luscious," Charlie said, smoothing her hands down her hips for effect. "And don't get me started on how well I beat my face. But do you think he even noticed?"

"Nope."

"Ding! Ding! Correct answer." Charlie shook her head. "He didn't even come with me to the damn luncheon. I just don't know what's been going on with us. There was a time when we were inseparable."

"Not to throw dirt in the mix, but how long have you two been together?"

"About two years now."

"And he's still your *boyfriend*?" Shivelle asked with a raised eyebrow.

"Mason was married before," Charlie said.

"To your best friend," Shivelle said.

She didn't say it in a malicious way, and her facial expression didn't suggest that she was being messy. However, she was just letting Charlie know that she knew what was up—which Charlie should have expected, since Shivelle knew Emerson first.

"Yes, and that whole situation was a mess, so I don't want to go into detail. But I will say they were already divorced when we started dating."

"I'm not judging. The man I'm seeing now is my ex's uncle." Shivelle gave a loud laugh. "Gerald thought he had seen the last of me, and then poof! I show up at Thanksgiving. But seriously, back to you. Regardless of if he was married before and who to, it's been two years."

"What are you saying?"

"That I've been around the block a few times. And if he isn't giving you time or commitment, then maybe there might be somebody else."

"Mason wouldn't cheat on me," she said, not sounding sure. "He loves me. He loves his family."

"Then why don't you have a ring on your finger?" Shivelle quizzed. "And if you aren't getting his time and attention, he's putting it somewhere else."

"There is the female detective at his job. She's pretty, but he says there's nothing going on," Charlie said. "But then again, he also never even told me that she was a woman, and he's with her every day. I–I walked in on them not too long ago."

"Doing what?" Shivelle asked, wide-eyed.

"Nothing. She was just too close to him, leaned over with her titties all in his face, girl. Like this." Charlie leaned over and shook her cleavage before standing back up. "I almost slapped that bitch. But that's the Baltimore in me. The Elegant in me told me to just play my cards. But there was something about the way she looked at him when she smiled. Like a girl with a crush."

"Baby, forget that. That woman would have been laid out on the ground messing with me," Shivelle said.

"I just hope that after I showed up there, she sees that he has a woman at home."

"Times have changed, Charlie," Shivelle said, giving her a knowing look. "These women now don't care if a man is taken or married. They see how good he treats you and don't think to themselves, 'I want a man like him.' No. They think, 'I want *him*.' So, don't for one second think that floozy is going to let up on something she wants just because you have it. Do you love your man?"

"Of course I do."

"Then the first course of action is getting him involved with your business. The second is to watch that bitch and make sure she stays in her place. I like you, Charlie, I really do. But I'll be the first to tell you that if things aren't good at home, then they can only be okay in business. Get your house in order."

"You mean put my foot down?"

"Exactly. And I don't mean telling him that you don't want him talking to her, because if he works with her, he'll have to. I'm talking about using some of that Baltimore girl magic I know you have and having a discussion with Detective Slut."

"Detective Slut?" MJ's voice sounded from out of nowhere as he repeated what Shivelle said.

"Aht! MJ, we don't say those words," Charlie said through her laughter. She turned her attention back to

Shivelle and nodded her head. "I get where you're coming from, but that woman has no loyalty to me. If there's
one thing I've learned is that a bitch will only do as much
as you allow her to. My beef is with Mason, and Mason
alone. Matter of fact, when I leave here, I'm going to have
some words with him. It's time he put some respect on
my name!"

"I heard the hell out of that, darling!" Shivelle said.
"Let's wrap things up here so you can get out of here."

And wrap things up was exactly what they did. Within
fifteen minutes, Charlie and MJ were on their way back
home. She played scenarios in her head about what she
would say and what would happen. She even acted some
out as she drove.

"'I don't want you talking to that bitch anymore!' No,
that's too much," she told herself and tried again. "'I
know that ho likes you. Fire her!' Okay, Charlie, tone it
down a little."

She role-played with herself until she was pulling
into her driveway. The light to their bedroom was on,
so Charlie knew Mason was home. She took a sleeping
MJ out of his car seat and went inside the house. Her
first stop was MJ's bedroom, and she was pleased with
herself that she was able to put a fresh Pull-Up on him
and change him into his pajamas without him waking up.
When she was done with that, she knew it was showtime.

She could hear the suspenseful music playing in her
head as she walked to the master bedroom. She could
hear Mason clicking away at the keyboard on his laptop,
which meant he was noting a case, but she didn't care.
She was tired of being put second next to work. She
didn't care that he had the job before they were together.
There had to be compromise somewhere, and right then,
she guessed her name was Compromise.

"We need to talk," she said as soon as she opened the bedroom door. "So shut the damn laptop."

Mason, who was sitting up on the bed and under the covers with his laptop on his lap, looked up from the screen at her serious face. She could tell that he was exhausted, but once again, she didn't care. He did as she said and shut his laptop, although he didn't look too happy about it.

"I thought you said everything you needed to say to me earlier," Mason commented.

"I didn't say nearly enough earlier."

"What is it now then? You want to add how I'm probably fucking the neighbor too?"

"No, but I do want to talk about Detective Sl—I mean Lawson," Charlie said, crossing her arms. "I don't trust her. She likes you, Mason, and I can tell that she's the type who's used to getting whatever she wants. I can't get how she was leaning over and smiling at you out of my head. It was like a cheetah preparing to pounce on her prey. I know I can't tell you to fire her, but if you can put some distance between the two of you at work, I think that would be best."

Charlie was beyond surprised at the words that had just come out of her mouth. Her mind was yelling for her to call Detective Lawson all kinds of mean names, but she didn't. She'd taken the high road.

"I agree with you one hundred percent," he said.

"Don't argue with me on this—Wait, what?" She gave him a puzzled look.

"I'm saying that I agree with you," he said again. "And I've already told Detective Lawson that her behavior has been unorthodox and if it continues, she will no longer have a job."

"You told her that?"

"Yes, I did."

"But why?"

"Because there is no one on this earth that can jeopardize this thing I've built with the love of my life."

"The love of your life, huh?" Charlie scoffed. "I haven't been feeling much of that. You've been really dropping the ball as my man lately, Mason. I mean, aren't I a good woman to you? Don't I deserve the same support as I give?"

"You're the most amazing woman I have ever come across in my life," Mason said, getting out of bed. He walked over and took Charlie by the hands. "I do support you. I'm sorry about what I said earlier about your designs being a hobby. I know what they mean to you, and from now on, I'll be better at proving that."

"How?"

"What, you want me to try on the dresses to make sure they look right? Because I will!"

"No!" Charlie laughed. "I don't think that's a good idea."

"You might be right about that," Mason said, joining in on her laughter. "But I'm serious. Anything you need, I got you, babe. I can even try and pull a few strings to get you an investor."

"That's what I kind of need to talk to you about," Charlie told him with a twinkle in her eye. "Remember a while back that event I went to with Emerson? Well, I met an investor. Shivelle Stine!"

"Shivelle Stine, as in *the* Shivelle Stine?" Mason asked with wide eyes.

"Yes!" Charlie was beaming. "She loved the idea for Elegant, and she invested in my dream to be a world-renowned dress designer. We recently picked a store location, and if everything goes well, we should be open before you know it. Soon everybody will know who Charlie Dixon is."

"Whoa! Baby, that's amazing," Mason said and hugged her tightly. "I'm so happy for you. Why didn't you tell me this? Especially with what I said earlier. You should have thrown that in my face and made me look stupid."

"Because I wanted your support to be real, not because you see me making it," Charlie said, blinking her tears away. "I just wanted you to be proud of me, and of the family we've made together. I'm sorry if I'm a little bold and my attitude is a little loud sometimes, but I work so hard. But none of that means anything when you don't notice. But this? This was the first thing I've ever done for myself and by myself. Still, it's pointless if I don't have you beside me."

"Well, I'm here, baby, and I'm not going anywhere. In fact, I'm going to be home a lot more. And I think I'm going to cool it on the overtime hours for a while. Especially if my baby is about to be a millionaire dress designer. I think we can afford it."

His grin was contagious, and Charlie found herself smiling like an idiot. She stepped on her tip toes and kissed him deeply. She was happy that the conversation hadn't taken the terrible left turn she thought it might.

Suddenly, she pulled away from him, and Mason stared at her like something was wrong.

"If you're serious, are you sure they're going to be okay with you not being at work as much? And what about Jewel's case?"

"Unfortunately, it's looking like we don't have any leads." Mason shook his head and looked away briefly. "The only thing we know is that the murder was personal. But my boss is telling us we need to focus on other cases that we can solve. I'll have to tell Mikayla that I'm sorry."

"Damn," Charlie said, shaking her head. "That's tough. But I think things would be different if she had actually been close to Jewel."

"Yeah, let's make a pact to always be there for MJ no matter what," Mason said and pulled her close. "I don't want him growing up with resentment toward either one of us."

"He won't, because he has two terrific parents raising him."

"Oh, so now you think I'm terrific," he teased her.

"No, I think *this* is terrific," she teased back and let her hand fall inside the crotch area of his pajama pants. She stroked his manhood until she felt it wake up. "You like that, huh?"

"Hell yeah," he breathed.

"You ain't been giving my dick away, have you?"

"Hell no," he moaned as she stroked.

"Good, because I want to suck it. Can I?"

"Yeah," he told her and watched her drop to her knees.

It had been a while since she tasted him on her tongue, and she was craving him. She pulled down his pants and stared his one-eyed monster in the face. It was so thick and chocolate, she almost couldn't help herself. She devoured him whole, sucking and slurping on his dick like a Push Pop. You would have thought she was making a porno the way she was giving him head, and he was in heaven. When his legs started to shake, he'd had enough, and he pulled his dick out of her mouth.

"My turn," he said.

Mason scooped Charlie up in his arms, turned off the lights, and laid her down on the bed. He took his time removing her clothes, and it amazed Charlie how well he knew her body even in the dark. He maneuvered her like a pro, and when she felt his face between her legs, she let a happy cry escape her lips.

She closed her eyes and quivered when his tongue made its first lick. She made her mind up. She was going to give him the benefit of the doubt and enjoy a night of passionate sex. She just hoped that this time, he followed through on his promises.

Chapter 15

Mikayla

If it hadn't been for her lawyer, Mikayla would have been a train wreck. Charles trying to get custody of the girls had completely put a thorn in her heel, and that was exactly what he wanted it to do. The next divorce mediation came a few weeks after Jewel's burial, and Mikayla hadn't seen or heard from Damian. He left right after the service, and she didn't know where he was. She'd been used to not seeing him before, but now things were different. Now her daughters constantly asked when they were going to see him again, and she wished she had an answer for them. But the honest answer was that she didn't know. Her main focus was on making sure that her scandalous husband didn't stand a chance in a custody battle.

"Mr. Avery, are you aware that your client is suing my client for full custody?" Mikayla's lawyer, Sarah Winters, said to Charles's lawyer, Peter Avery.

They'd decided to meet in the board room of Sarah's firm. Mikayla and her counsel were on one side of the table, while Charles and his counsel sat on the other. Sarah was an older white lady who wore her graying blonde hair in a short cut with a side bang. Mr. Avery was about fifteen years her junior, but as sharp as a whistle. He wore his short brown hair combed back, and always had a spiffy suit on when Mikayla saw him. She could see why he'd gone into the business of lawyering. He was damned good at his job.

"Yes, I'm fully aware," Mr. Avery said, nodding his head. "My client feels that for the safety of his children, they should be with him. Your client has forgotten them at school on more than one occasion, and also her pill addiction. If you are willing to go to court, then we are ready to make all of this public knowledge.

"And, Mrs. King, you're a very popular woman these days. How would your supporters feel knowing that your daughters tell their therapist they're scared you won't wake up one day? Because if we go to court, that's exactly what will happen. We are prepared to call Dr. Barnes to the stand."

Mikayla swallowed hard. When Charles told her the girls had said they'd seen a pill bottle in her bathroom, she'd almost fainted. It was true she had a bottle of pain medication in her bathroom cabinet, but she didn't take any of them. She almost did, but she stopped herself. After he'd said that to her, she took the entire pill bottle to her lawyer and told her what had happened. She was terrified she was going to lose custody of her children because of a little moment of weakness, but Sarah had told her not to worry, even though that proved to be impossible.

"*If* my client does decide to go to court, you can bring those details up all you wish," Sarah said to Mr. Avery. She went in the folder in front of her and pulled out a stapled packet. "But I should warn you that if you do, then you should be ready for the public to also see all of Mrs. King's hospital records since she's been married to Mr. King. Multiple broken bones and several photos of Mrs. King with black eyes going years back."

"Mrs. King never pressed charges on Mr. King for any of those incidents."

"Maybe, but it's painfully obvious how she got hurt all of those times. And who is going to give a domestic abuser custody of two little girls?" Sarah said with a smirk. "You see, even with whatever evidence you *think* you have on my client, nothing is as heavy as the load as the one Mr. King created for himself. Do yourself a favor and drop the suit. We're here to get the two of them divorced without getting the courts involved."

Mikayla held her breath as Mr. Avery and Charles huddled together. They were whispering, so she couldn't make out their words, but she could read Charles's facial expressions. She'd been married to him for years and could tell by the way he was clenching his jaw that he wasn't happy with what his lawyer was saying. In the end, he just nodded and turned back to face Mikayla and Sarah.

"My client has made a decision." Mr. Avery cleared his throat. "He has agreed to drop the custody suit and meet in exactly one month's time to make the final arrangements for the divorce. Hopefully then we can all come to terms that we can agree on."

Mikayla felt a whoosh of relief come over her, but she kept her cool. She tried to act like she knew he was going to drop the suit all along, but in truth, she didn't know *what* was going to happen that day. Sarah had told her to trust her, and now Mikayla knew not to ever question her lawyering skills again.

Sarah and Mr. Avery wrapped up a few things before he exited with Charles. Mikayla didn't see, because she was too busy grinning at Sarah, but she felt Charles's glare on the side of her face until he was out of the room.

"Thank you so much," Mikayla said, shaking Sarah's hand. "You're a lifesaver."

"You're more than welcome," Sarah said, offering her a kind smile. "Men like him always go for the low blows.

I knew his game, though. He never wanted to take those kids from you, but they were his way to break you at the foundation. That way, he could offer you pennies to settle on as long as he let you have custody of the girls. But that wasn't flying on my watch."

Mikayla recognized something in her voice. She wasn't speaking just as a lawyer with facts. There was emotion behind her words.

"You talk like you know my struggle personally, Sarah."

"Just because my life is calm now doesn't mean I haven't gone through any storms," Sarah said in a matter-of-fact tone. "My ex-husband was the same way. Abusive, controlling, and in the end, he tried to take the kids. Back then, I wasn't able to afford a lawyer, so he almost got everything, and I would have been on the streets."

"So what happened then?"

"It came out that he'd fathered two other children while we were married, and neither of the women knew about each other or that he was married. One of them even had a similar story of abuse as me. I ended up getting everything, and the son of a bitch is still paying me alimony."

"Well, let's just hope I have the same kind of success story," Mikayla said, standing.

"With me by your side, you will." Sarah winked and got up as well to walk Mikayla to the door. "Let's just hope they don't try to stall us out any more than they already have. I'm sure you're ready to have Birmingham back as your last name."

"You're right about that!"

"I'll be in touch soon so we can figure out a day that works best for all of us."

Mikayla gave her well wishes for the rest of the day and went on about her own. On her way out of the firm, she pulled her phone out of her purse to check and make sure that the babysitter hadn't called. She didn't have any missed calls from the babysitter, but she did have a few texts from Brandon.

The relationship with detective Brandon Janes had been steadily growing. Mikayla found herself thinking of him more often as of late. She didn't want to admit it, but she was beginning to fall for him.

I miss you, beautiful.

Call me when you get a chance. I need to hear your voice.

She smiled to herself. Now that the mediation was over, her anxiety had calmed down. She could try to enjoy life a little. Brandon was still working on Jewel's case, but in between time, he had been working on Mikayla too. She didn't remember the last time she opened herself up to someone, but with Brandon, it just felt natural. As Mikayla read his texts, she felt the butterflies in her stomach go haywire. He definitely had her on a cloud, and she didn't want to come down. She hoped nothing would change between them when they finally slept together, because Mikayla for sure felt the sexual tension between them heating up.

She decided he could wait for her phone call until she got to her car. Before she got there, however, her phone began to ring. She smiled, thinking it was Brandon, but when she looked at the caller ID, she saw someone else's name.

"Hello?" She answered on the third ring.

"Hey, sis." Damian's deep voice came in from the other end of the phone.

"You're just gonna 'hey, sis' me when I haven't seen or heard from you in weeks? You just left and didn't say anything to anyone."

"Yeah, I did," Damian said and paused.

"So, you don't have anything to say for yourself?" Mikayla asked, walking through the tall double glass doors of the firm into the cold, brisk air.

"Listen, I didn't mean to just leave like that." Damian sighed. "Some things just came up. You know how it is."

"Actually, I don't," Mikayla said flatly and then let out a small huff of air. "The girls have been asking about you."

"Yeah?"

"Yeah. I don't know what kind of spell you put on my babies, but they love you. And—" She paused briefly. "Damian, look. I know we have some crazy rifts to get through, and maybe you'll never forgive me for not coming to visit you while you were locked up. We both had our own ways of dealing with it, and I can only hope that you understand that. But the truth is that we're family, and all we have is each other now."

"You have more than just me," Damian pointed out.

"Well, I want you too," Mikayla said. When she realized she really meant what she said, she smiled. She reached her car and hurried to get in and start it for some warm air. "And I want you to know that from now on, you have me too. You don't have to be alone."

"Thanks," Damian said and grew quiet.

His silence lasted so long that Mikayla had to check her phone to make sure they were still connected. When she saw that the time was still going, she placed the phone back to her ear. She could hear him breathing, and she cleared her throat.

"So, are you at least still in Baltimore?"

"For the time being."

"Well, I would love it if you would come to dinner tomorrow night, if you don' have anything else to do. The girls would love to see you."

"I'll see if I can fit it in my schedule."

Mikayla wanted to ask him what the hell he could be doing, but she fought the urge.

"Okay, perfect," she said instead. "It will start at seven thirty. I hope you can make it."

"Me too," he said. "There was a reason I was calling you. Have you talked to your friend's detective boyfriend about the case?"

"No, I haven't. But I've been working with another detective, Detective Janes. He says they're getting closer to finding out who murdered Jewel, which is good, because I'm ready for this all to be officially over."

"He told you that?" Damian asked.

"Yeah, he will be at dinner tomorrow if you want to ask him a few questions yourself."

"You know what? I do. As a matter of fact, I'll be at the dinner tomorrow."

"For sure?"

"Yeah, I don't see why not. I've been thinking about my nieces too."

"Great! They'll be happy to see you."

"And Mikayla—"

Beep! Beep!

An incoming call interrupted what he was about to say. When Mikayla looked at the caller ID, she saw Brandon's contact on the screen. She almost squealed like a schoolgirl from excitement. She loved how he chased her. It was refreshing to feel wanted.

"Damian, I'm going to have to call you back. I have an important call on the other line." She clicked over before giving him a chance to say goodbye.

"Hello?"

"I'm glad to know you're still alive," Brandon joked.

"I'm sorry. I was wrapped up in there with my soon-to-be ex-husband and our lawyers going over everything."

"It's okay, baby."

The way he said "baby" gave her chills. His voice was so smooth and sexy.

"How did everything go with that?" he asked. "I know it's something you were worried about."

"Let's just say that by the time my lawyer was finished with him, it looked like Charles had been chewed and spit out," Mikayla said.

"So, things went better than expected, then?"

"More than that. He dropped the entire custody suit."

"That's music to my ears," Brandon said, sounding relieved. "I couldn't believe he was trying to do that anyways. I hate when men take out their masculinity issues on other people just because they don't know if they like themselves or not."

"That sounds like a real personal problem to me," Mikayla said. "Anyways, how was your day in the office?"

Her car had finally heated up to her liking, and she pulled away from the curb. She figured she might as well go to the store while she still had a sitter, instead of doing everything last minute the next day. She figured the best food for that spread was pasta, and she tried to decide if she wanted to make spaghetti or chicken alfredo while she listened to Brandon talk.

"Same ol', same ol'," he said. "Another day of people acting like they don't have any damn sense at all."

"I bet." She giggled. "How is it working with Mason as your boss?"

"I don't see him much. Let's just say I keep my nose clean and get all my work done so I don't have to talk to him unless I have to."

"I understand."

"Do you? You went from being a stay-at-home mom to a stay-at-home boss. You've never had to answer to a higher-up at work," he joked.

"Yeah, but I had a dictator as a husband," she reminded him, though she didn't really want to talk about that, so she changed the subject quickly. "Are you still coming over for dinner tomorrow night?"

"Of course. Why wouldn't I be?"

"Because you're scared to meet my little monsters," Mikayla teased.

"Please. If they are anything like you, then they can't be little monsters," he said with a chuckle. "But no, I'm not afraid to meet them. I deal with the worst of the worst on a daily basis. I'm not scared of a couple little girls."

"We'll see," Mikayla said. "My brother is going to be joining us too. Is that all right?"

"Damian? Your house, your rules. You inviting me to a family dinner—are you trying to tell me something?"

"Nothing that you don't already know," Mikayla said.

"Enlighten me."

Mikayla felt her face grow warm. Even though Brandon was nowhere near her, he made her shy. Her feelings for him grew every time she talked to him, and she couldn't deny it.

"You've been so consistent these past weeks, and I just want to show you that I appreciate your efforts, that's all. Is that so bad?"

"No . . . that sounds really good," Brandon said, suddenly sounding distracted.

Mikayla heard a shout in the background and what sounded like a struggle.

"Is everything all right?" she asked, concerned.

"Everything is fine, baby. They just brought someone in who's a fighter. Actually, let me attend to this, and I'll just see you tomorrow night."

"Okay. I'll see you then," she said and kissed the phone.

He made a kiss sound in the receiver before he hung up.

Mikayla was higher than high. She was falling for him, and there was no turning back. However, there was one decision she still needed to make, and that was when to tell her best friends about him. She didn't feel the need to rush, because Charlie had hidden her relationship with Mason, and Emerson had hid two situations from them. So, why not keep some of her own business to herself until she was ready? Plus, she didn't want to hear any warnings about how she was moving too fast. She had a happiness inside of her that had been foreign for ages, and she just wanted have it for as long as she could.

Chapter 16

Emerson

Emerson felt like she was trapped in a bad dream, but it was her real life. She'd been sleeping with Jacob and doing unexplainable nasty things to his niece, who she later learned was his eldest brother's daughter. The two had been raised more like close cousins than uncle and niece, since Jacob wasn't that much older than her.

After the luncheon, Emerson almost had a breakdown. Her guilt felt overwhelming. On one end, she didn't feel like she was wrong, because she was entitled to date whomever she wanted. But on the other end, Cali was still his niece. No matter how she tried to spin it in her head, she always came out the bad guy. In the end, Emerson made the decision to just not tell him, and she hoped Cali would keep it to herself as well.

Emerson decided to stop answering and returning her calls. She figured it would be best to just let that situation fizzle out and die.

The only good that came out of the situation was that it gave Emerson a real chance to take a step back and see how self-destructive she was. It dawned on her that not everything she wanted was good for her, and the choices she'd been making were poor ones. Like, for instance, the fact that she and Jacob hadn't taken things up a notch. It suddenly became silly that she'd been keeping a good man at bay just because she was afraid to let him in. But the truth was, she'd already opened the doors. She'd played with the thought of cutting both Jacob and Cali off, but when the thought of Jacob not being in her life anymore made her sick to her stomach, she knew it was time to stop playing before she lost him for real.

Almost immediately following the luncheon, her attitude changed, and Jacob didn't hide that he noticed. They were on a movie date one night, and while Emerson was buttering the popcorn, she noticed a few women eyeing Jacob like they wanted to butter him. There was one in particular—light skin, long hair, and a big old booty. She stood out the most because she was the one being the most thirsty. She didn't hide that she was interested and even left her friends standing in the concessions line to approach Jacob. Once Emerson saw that, she beelined it over to stand next to him, thinking that would stop the woman's advance. It didn't.

"Excuse me. I was over there with my girls, and I couldn't help but notice you over here," she said, completely ignoring Emerson standing there. "My name is Jasmine, and I just want to let you know you're the finest man I've ever seen. Take my number and call me later? We can have some fun if you want."

Jacob's mouth dropped at her forwardness, and it was obvious that he was tongue-tied. Emerson, on the other hand, was seeing red. How dare that big-booty tramp come up to her date and disrespect her? If they were in a cartoon, Jasmine would be able to see the smoke coming from Emerson's ears. She'd definitely stop looking at Jacob like she wanted to bone him right then and there.

"*Excuse me.*" Emerson started by mocking her, and that got Jasmine's attention real quick. "I know you didn't just come up and start flirting with *my* man in front of me."

"And if I did?" Jasmine said, rolling her neck.

Emerson forgot everything she'd been learning in therapy. It all just flew away from her, kind of like her fist did when she hit Jasmine square in the jaw. The young woman stumbled back, dazed that Emerson had actually hit her. Emerson was shocked too, but she didn't back down.

"When you see him, just know that's all me, baby." She puffed her chest out. "And now you know what happens when you fuck with something that's mine."

She suddenly felt Jacob grab her hand and pull her out of the movie theater. At first, she didn't know why they were leaving if they hadn't seen their movie. But on their way out, they saw security headed to where they just were. Their walk turned into a run as they rushed to the car like bad middle school kids.

"You trying to get us arrested, woman?" Jacob exclaimed breathlessly. He pulled his Audi Q5 out of the movie theater parking lot. "Who would have thought Emerson the superstar would have such a powerful right hook?"

"She was all up on my boyfriend. What was I supposed to do?"

"Boyfriend?" He raised his brow and glanced over at her from the driver's seat. "Who are you, and what have you done with Emerson?"

"I'm right here, silly." She giggled, her adrenaline pumping. "I guess I've just put a few things into perspective."

"Oh, yeah? Like what?"

"Like exactly how much you mean to me," she said and she saw the alarmed expression on his face soften. "You've been nothing but patient with me, and I've done nothing but shove you away."

"It's okay, baby. I understand. You've been through a lot."

"Just because you understand doesn't mean it's okay."
She shook her head and opened her mouth to talk again,
but then shut it. She grew frustrated because she couldn't
find the words she wanted to say. "I've never done this
before, so bear with me."

"Take your time, babe."

"It's just . . . I've been so used to only showing the world
eighty percent of myself, because I was always ashamed
of the other twenty percent. I couldn't show the world
crazy Emerson. I had to be perfect all the time just so everyone would think I was okay. But then you came alone,
and it just felt good to be not okay with someone who
could put me back together again," Emerson said. By that
time, she was crying. "And it *feels* really great to be with
someone who can help me turn that eighty and twenty
into a one hundred percent. I'm so transparent with you,
and it comes so fluently, and I think that's what scares
me. Knowing that you're the one for me. So, if you'll still
have me, I would love to turn what we have into a serious
commitment. I mean, if that's what you want, anyway."

Jacob gave Emerson no warning before he swerved
over to the side of the road. It was a good thing she was
wearing her seatbelt, because she would have probably
gotten a serious case of whiplash from the abrupt stop.
At first, she was afraid that she'd said something wrong,
but when he reached over to pull her into the deepest kiss
they'd ever shared, she knew she'd said something right.

"Of course that's what I want," he said when he released her from the kiss. He cupped her chin with one of
his hands and stared into her soul. "Ever since I saw you
in that courtroom, I knew you would be mine one day,
Emerson Dayle."

"I'm changing my last name back to Leighton." She
spoke softly. "I don't want you to call me by another
man's name."

"Don't. It's a part of your past, and that's not something that bothers me. Plus, when you do change your last name, it will be to Andrews. Mark my words."

"I might hold you to that, but for now, we can just take it a day at a time."

And they did. By letting go of the reigns, Emerson opened herself up to a different kind of joy she didn't think she could experience. She was in love, and she could finally admit it. She didn't have to hide it, and she could scream it to the highest mountaintops. She was so high on her horse that in the coming weeks, she'd almost forgotten all about Cali. That was, until she ran into her.

It was a cold winter evening, and Jacob had come down with a cold and was acting like the biggest baby ever. Emerson had enough of his whining, so she ran to the store for cough medicine. As she walked down the aisle for medicine, her phone pinged, and of course, it was a message from Jacob.

Babyyy. Hurry up. I need you. I think I'm on my last leg.

She found herself grinning. He was so dramatic. All he had was a common cold, and he was acting like it was the end of the world. She'd hate to see how he acted if he were really sick.

"You're smiling like you just hit the jackpot."

The voice brought a cold sweat to Emerson's back. She didn't have to turn around to know who was behind her—and the fact that she knew who the voice belonged to was the reason she didn't want to turn around. Sure enough, there was Cali, standing there wearing a white bubble coat and holding a loaf of bread in her hands.

"Cali, what are you doing here?"

"Um, what does it look like?" Cali said, holding up the loaf of bread. "I'm grocery shopping. Looks like you're here to get Unc some medicine."

"And how would you know that?"

"I talked to him earlier this morning. He told me he had a cold, but you were taking good care of him. I should have told him how good you used to take care of me," she said, flashing a cunning smile.

"Cali, please don't."

"Why, whatever do you mean?" Cali asked, feigning innocence.

"You know what I mean. I don't have to tell you, because you know *exactly* what you're doing."

"Do I?"

"Okay, enough with the games," Emerson said in an exhausted voice.

"You're the only one playing games. You just cut me off with no warning," Cali said.

Emerson could hear the hurt in her voice. "Cali, you and I both know why I had to cut things off. I might not have done it in the best way, but it had to be done. I had no idea that you were Jacob's niece. It caught me completely by surprise."

"And you chose him over me. I get it."

"It wasn't like that."

"So, if I weren't his niece, then you would still be fucking me, right?"

"Maybe, but—"

"Then that means you chose him over me," Cali repeated.

"Okay, yes, I did," Emerson said, giving in. "But not because you aren't a good person, because you are."

"Then what is it? I know you liked me. And I know you love having sex with me. You played me."

"What we had was fun, but that's all it was. And you can cut the crap. You and I both know that you had to have known Jacob was seeing me. I told you about my luncheon weeks before it happened."

"I didn't know that you would be his date!" Cali exclaimed, and an elderly couple passing by turned and gave them evil stares before continuing on their way. They both realized they were getting loud, and began speaking in a whisper.

"I thought I would be coming to surprise you, but instead, I'm the one who got surprised. You know, I was really starting to like you."

"Cali, I'm sorry if I hurt you. I really am. But I want to be with Jacob," Emerson said, holding her palms out like she didn't know what to do. "I just don't want this to end up like the last time I was involved with a woman. Hopefully we can keep this a secret between us."

"And how much are you willing to pay to keep my mouth closed?"

"Whatever amount you want." Emerson didn't miss a beat.

Cali studied her face to see if she was serious. Emerson prepared for her to say some crazy number, but whatever it was, Emerson was ready to pay it.

"You really love Unc, huh?"

"Yes, I do." Emerson sighed. "The last five years of my life have been spent trying to figure out where I belong, where I fit in, and what makes me happy. I found all of those answers within one person. Jacob takes me to a place that nobody has ever taken me. I don't have to hide myself with him. He accepts every piece of me, and he's a good man. I will gladly pay any price to protect his heart."

Emerson's voice shook as she spoke, but that was because she felt every word. She would do and pay anything to keep Jacob from finding out the truth. A blow like that would crush him, and she would lose him.

"That was beautiful, but not beautiful enough to not warrant some kind of payment," Cali said, smirking. "How about you pay for a five-day vacation for me and a friend to go to Jamaica and we can call it even?"

"That's all?" Emerson asked. She couldn't believe it.

"Yes, that's all."

"But why?"

"You were right about one thing. Uncle Jacob is a good guy. One of the best I've ever met. He's gotten me out of trouble more times than I'd care to name, and the last thing I want to do is break his heart. I haven't seen him this happy in a long time, and I know why. I *am* going to miss our long nights of lovemaking, but I guess I'll always have the memories."

"You . . . didn't record any of it, did you?" Emerson asked, almost scared to know the answer.

"Hell no!" Cali made a face. "I don't leave a digital trail of where my pussy has been."

"Good."

"I want my tickets by the end of the week," Cali said, pointing her finger at Emerson as she walked away. "I'll stop by and—"

"No!" Emerson said quickly. "I'll just send you your itinerary via email. I think it might be best if you stayed away for at least a little while. Just until things aren't so awkward."

"Good point," Cali said and shot Emerson a sad smile. "See you around, Eme."

Emerson watched Cali walk away. With each step she took, Emerson felt a little more life come back into her. She felt a release of good energy overcome her. If Cali kept her word, Emerson wouldn't have anything to worry about. She could finally close the ending chapter to her last story and start a new book.

Chapter 17

Damian

Damian lay on his back, still, as he read a small note-book. The day of Mikayla's dinner had come, and he had his own reasons to be eager for it. But something else weighed heavier on his mind. It was what Jewel had left for him to find.

A little before Mason had come into of the apartment, Damian had checked where Oddie had directed him to look. Inside the bathroom ceiling vent was a small box, in which Jewel had left a small notepad and a cell phone. She'd used it to document the last six months of her life. It was like Damian was getting to know his mom, really getting to know her, for the first time over the past few weeks. One of her passages caught his attention every time he opened the notepad.

> *I thought it would feel like I'm washing away my own past sins when I clean the blood in these houses. But really it just makes me remember all the wrongs I've done. I was a bad mother. I wonder if I can ever make it right.*

He didn't know what she meant by "make it right." Maybe she was talking about the diamond, but he read the book front to back, and Jewel didn't make mention of a single diamond. He'd hoped that she would have

said where she stashed it and that was why she wanted
him to find the notepad. But that was wishful thinking.
The phone Jewel left was no good either, because it had
a passcode on it. He'd tried her birthday and his own
birthday, but it didn't work. He only had one more time
to try to unlock the phone before it locked indefinitely.
He felt like a hamster on a wheel. No matter what he
found, he was still left in the same place.

"What did you want me to find, Mama?" Damian said
out loud, flipping the small book to the part that started
when she was in Baltimore. "The only thing here is—"

He sat up straight, flipping the pages slowly. His eyes
grew big when he got to the final page. He'd been so
focused looking at her thoughts and for a clue about the
diamond that everything else fell to the wayside, but not
now. He was desperate and giving even ink blotches a
second glance. At the bottom right hand corner of the
last page was a set of four numbers, and next to it was
the name of a school. Under the school, there was the
name of what looked like a nightclub, Winx. But the
school stood out, because there was a heart around it.

"Douglas Private School?" He pondered to himself.
"And what are these numbers for?"

His eyes fell on the cell phone that was lying beside him
on the bed. Had she left the code for him to find? There
was only one way to find out. He picked up the phone and
powered it on. He figured that even if he got locked out of
the device, he wasn't going to get in it anyway.

"Seven, eight, three, three," he said as he pressed the
digits on the keypad.

He heard a soft click, and the phone screen lit up. He
was in! The first place he checked was her call log, and he
dialed the last number she had called.

"Douglas Private School. This is Melody. How may I
help you today?"

Damian disconnected the phone quickly and sat up. What interest did Jewel have with a private school? Had she hidden the diamond there? He researched the location of the school, and when he found it, he made a decision to make a visit. Within the hour, he was showered, dressed, and out the door.

The school turned out to be on the same side of town as Mikayla's home, and when Damian arrived, he parked on the curb. He stared at the school for a few moments. It was so large that he couldn't tell what grade levels it held. For all he knew, it could have been a school for misbehaved children.

He got out of his car and tucked his hands inside his coat pockets as he headed for the door. On his way inside, he passed a few teachers with papers and books in their hands. They gave him curious glances, but he paid them no mind. He was there to find out his mother's interest in the place, not fall victim to their condescending looks.

Once he was buzzed in, Damian was slightly taken aback. He'd never gone to a school that looked as fancy as Douglas. It was two stories with crystal chandeliers hanging from the ceiling, and the marble on the floors had tiny specs of shine in it.

Damian made his way to the office where he was greeted by the secretary. Her nametag read Melody, and he knew she was the one who had answered the phone when he called.

"May I help you?" she asked sweetly. She was a cute, petite lady with smooth cocoa skin and maybe in her late forties. He paused, realizing he hadn't thought about what he was going to say. She gave him an encouraging smile.

"Uh," he started and cleared his throat. "Was my mother here recently?"

"It depends on who your mother is, sweetheart," she said. "Do you have a picture?"

"Yeah, here," Damian said and pulled a photo of him and Jewel from his wallet. "That's her."

"Oh, Jewel!" The secretary's face lit up. "Such a sweetheart. She came to visit the girls a few times."

"The girls?"

"Yes, Zuri and Kai. They loved having their grandmother here, especially since she brought treats every time she came."

"Zuri and Kai? This is their school?"

"Well, yeah." Melody gave him a funny look. "Why else would Jewel have come?"

Damian was even more confused. Since when had Jewel gotten close to Zuri and Kai? He knew Mikayla couldn't have known about it. She still had ill feelings about Jewel in the end.

"You all right?" Melody asked.

"Yeah, just wrapping my head around a few things," Damian said, nodding his head. "Did she say anything the last time she was here?"

"Just that she wanted to say goodbye since she wouldn't be in town for Kai's birthday next month."

"Thank you," Damian said and turned to leave.

"Tell Jewel I said hello when you talk to her, will you?" Melody asked.

When he looked over his shoulder to tell her that Jewel had died, he stopped himself. There was something about the happiness in her smile. He simply nodded his head and kept it pushing.

Damian had read somewhere that it was rude to show up to dinner emptyhanded, so when he rang Mikayla's doorbell, he had a bottle of wine in his hand. He was dressed casually in a pair of jeans and a sweater with a pair of Timberland boots on his feet. When she opened the door, he held out the bottle. She took the bottle and made way for him to enter.

"Come in, come in," she said, ushering him inside. "The girls are in the dining room, helping me set the table. I didn't tell them you were coming."

She shut the door behind him, and Damian inched his way toward the dining room. When he was in the doorway, he saw his beautiful nieces putting plates on the table. Kai saw him first and let out a thrilled shriek before running and hugging him.

"Uncle Damian! You came back," she said, squeezing him tight.

"Of course I did, kid," he said and hugged her back.

Zuri was putting up a tough front and had her arms crossed in front of her. She shot him a dirty look and tapped her foot.

"Well?" she asked.

"Well what?"

"I'm waiting for an apology!" she told her uncle. "You literally left without a word and you just came in our lives. Just like Grandma."

"I didn't mean to. There's just a lot of stuff I gotta figure out. But I can promise to always say goodbye before I leave."

"And call." She made one eye bigger than the other and pointed a quick finger at him.

"And call," he said with a smile.

"Okay." She smiled back and joined her sister by giving him a bear hug. "We missed you. Now we don't have anyone to sneak us extra dessert."

"I knew my snack drawer was getting emptied out faster than usual." Mikayla's voice came from behind them.

Kai's and Zuri's eyes grew wide. They let go of Damian and made a beeline for the exit. He couldn't help but to laugh.

"Yeah, y'all better run. And while you're at it, change out of your school uniforms before you eat," Mikayla called after them. She turned to Damian and put her hands on her hips. "I don't know why they like you so much."

"Probably because they've never had an uncle before." Damian shrugged. "Charles have siblings?"

"A sister," she answered and set the wine he'd brought on the table. "And I hate that bitch. I wouldn't let her around my kids if my life depended on it."

"I rest my case," Damian said. "They're excited to have more family."

His mind fell to the information he'd found that day. He sat down at the table, and Mikayla noticed the troubled look on his face. Sitting across from him, she looked at him with concerned eyes.

"You all right, Damian? I mean, with all things considering."

"I don't know," Damian told her. "But I think there are some things that you need to know."

"What? Did something happen?" she asked. "It's about Jewel, isn't it?"

"Yes."

"Damian, I—"

"She was visiting the girls at their school." He interrupted whatever it was she was about to say.

"What did you just say?"

"Jewel was visiting the girls at school while she was here in Baltimore. I assumed you didn't know anything about that."

"No, hell no. I didn't know anything about that." Mikayla's face held a shocked, almost angry expression. "And how would you even know that?"

"I found her phone in her apartment."

"You went back to her apartment?"

"Yeah, that's where I've been staying until I figure out what to do with all of her stuff." Damian told the partial truth. "I called the last number she dialed, and it was Douglas Private School."

"What the hell was she doing going to see my kids?"

"Visiting with her grandkids," Damian said, giving Mikayla a hard stare. "I think . . . I think she started to feel really bad about how she raised us, you know? I think she was facing her demons, and maybe she thought that she could start over with the girls. Make it right."

"Behind my back."

"You probably would have shut her down if she asked you to see them," Damian pointed out and Mikayla was silent. "The secretary said the last time she went to see them, she was telling them goodbye. And telling them that she wouldn't be around for Kai's birthday."

"Do you think she knew . . ." Mikayla's voice trailed off, but Damian knew what she was getting at.

"Maybe."

"Maybe Brandon—I mean Detective Janes can use this information in his investigation. Maybe whoever killed her followed her home from the school. I know that neighborhood has cameras, all those bougie white people."

"No, don't tell him."

"But why not? I think he can really help."

"Just trust me on this one. This is something that should stay between family," Damian said.

Mikayla looked at him long and hard. "All right," she said and sighed. "It can stay between us. Come wash your hands so you can help me bring this food out."

And that he did. Mikayla had really outdone herself. Smothered chicken, homemade mashed potatoes, sweet corn, and honey rolls were on the menu that night. Damian could feel his mouth salivating just at the smell. He couldn't wait to eat, but they were still waiting on one more guest.

Damian grabbed a roll from the bowl on the table. "So, Brandon, huh?"

"What about him?"

"I mean, if you're on a first name basis then—"

"It could just be strictly business," Mikayla said, shooting him an annoyed look before letting out a frustrated breath. "Okay, we've been kind of dating. But what's it to you? You've only been decent to me for a few weeks. Don't pull the big brother card already."

"I'm just saying, I've never heard of a detective dating someone involved in his case."

"You were in jail most of your life, so I'm sure you haven't."

"I watched a lot of movies and read a lot of books," he said, ignoring her dig. "Just be careful."

"I will," she told him.

The doorbell rang.

"That's him!" she said and rushed to the hallway to look at herself in the mirror.

She adjusted her long sweater dress and smoothed down a few flyaway hairs on her head. When she was satisfied with her reflection, she went to open the door.

Damian watched as the man entered and handed her a bouquet of roses. Her smile was so bright it would have lit up the whole house if the lights went out. She shut the door behind him and brought him to meet Damian.

"This is Damian," she said. "Damian, this is Detective Janes."

"Please, call me Brandon," he said with a smile. "Nice to meet you."

He held his hand out for Damian to shake. Damian hesitated, but shook his hand. Brandon had the look of a man that was too smooth. The pretty boy type. The kind to get whatever he wanted with one flash of his pearly whites. And right then, he had Mikayla trapped in his spell.

Damian offered a forced smile. "Nice to meet you too," he said.

By then, the girls had come back to join them. They took their usual seats on the sides of Damian, and Brandon sat next to Mikayla. After blessing the food, they all dug in. It was so good that they were all halfway through their plates before they started to make small talk.

"So, Mikayla says that you're working on our mother's case?" Damian asked after swallowing a spoonful of potatoes.

"Yes, I am." Brandon nodded. "And might I add, I am so sorry for your loss. I know you were just starting to rebuild a relationship with her since your release from prison."

"Yeah, well. You win some, you lose some. And this was just one of those terrible losses," Damian said. "But hopefully you'll find whoever did this to her."

"Believe me, we're working hard on this case. We don't want anyone else to turn up like that because we didn't do the best we could the first time around."

"Hmmm." Damian nodded his head and went back to eating his food. He felt Brandon's eyes on him the entire time, but he didn't look up again right away.

Beside him, Kai had finished eating her food and pushed away from the table. Mikayla stopped her before she could get too far.

"Let me see that plate," she said with her eyebrow raised.

"*Mom,* I ate almost all of my food," Kai groaned and showed her.

"I was just checking," Mikayla said, smiling at her daughter's sass.

"Mom, I'm done too," Zuri said, holding up her own plate. "Can you come help me with the instructions on my homework assignment? It won't take long."

"All right, baby," Mikayla said and turned to Brandon. "Excuse me. I'll be right back."

"Take your time," Brandon told her. "I'm sure Damian and I can find something to talk about."

"I don't know if I should be worried," Mikayla said and got up from the table.

She followed behind her daughters, but when she was out of Brandon's eyesight, she looked at Damian and mouthed the word *behave.* He waited until she got upstairs to place his fork down and clasp his hands together.

"So, are you going to tell me who you really are, or are you gonna make me ask?"

Damian's question caught Brandon by surprise. He was in the middle of chewing a piece of chicken, but he set his fork down too.

"I don't get what you mean," he said, giving Damian a blank stare.

"You're gonna make me ask." Damian answered his own question. "Who are you?"

"I'm Brandon Janes, a detective for the—"

"Cut the shit." Damian cut him short. "I spoke with a real detective working my mama's case, and either you don't know what's going on at your job, or you don't work there at all. They've put a halt on the case, something about no leads. So, which one is it? I'm gonna go with you don't work there at all."

Damian watched Brandon's face closely. He saw the vein protrude slightly at his temple and noticed that

Brandon's blank stare had turned into a glare. Damian didn't know what Brandon's game plan was. Pretend to be somebody important to charm his way into Mikayla's bedroom?

"I guess you caught me," Brandon said, putting his hands up. "You can't blame me though, right? I mean, your sister? That's one fine-ass woman right there."

"You're sick," Damian said, turning his nose up in a disgusted fashion. "Only a sick fuck would use a situation like this to try and get some pussy."

Brandon laughed loudly and suddenly.

"What's funny?"

"The fact that you think I did all of this for some pussy," Brandon said, still smiling sinisterly.

"What did you do it for then?"

"I'm going to tell you a story," Brandon said, clasping his hands together. "About a young woman who came to the United States from Cuba. She had nothing. No family, no money and nowhere to go. She lucked up and met a man who she fell in love with and married. The ring he gave her had been in his family for more years than he even knew, and the value of it went beyond the physical. You see, his family obtained the ring during a riot in the slave times. It was a symbol of victory and strife. So you can understand how much it pained them to have to pawn the ring when things got tight for her family.

"With the money they got from pawning the ring, she was able to buy a sewing machine. With that sewing machine, she began to design clothes for plump women. Although she was more on the petite side, she never thought it was fair that bigger women didn't have the same options as her. She changed that, and soon her clothing business took off.

"It wasn't planned, but within five years, that woman from Cuba was richer than she could have ever imagined.

She was introduced to a whole new way of living. She attended the opera, ballets, and even went to fancy museums. In fact, it was at a museum that she came face to face with the ring she'd had to part ways with all those years ago. It was fate, so it was a no-brainer that she had to buy it back no matter the cost. And she did. For one hundred thousand dollars, the ring was hers again. Three generations later, do you know what that rare pink diamond is worth?"

"A million dollars," Damian said, looking at Brandon with disbelief.

"Bingo. But to me, the great great great grandson of that Cuban woman, it is priceless."

"Tyrant." Damian cut his eyes at the man before him.

The slow smile that crossed his face told Damian that he had guessed right. He no longer saw a man. He saw a monster, one who would do anything to ensure he got what he wanted.

Tyrant glowered back at Damian, and the aura around him darkened. The pleasant expression was now gone from his face.

He's as private as a ghost. Bone's words replayed in Damian's head. A ghost was right. Tyrant had been hiding in plain sight the whole time.

"Have you found my diamond, Damian?" Tyrant asked.

"No," Damian growled.

It was taking everything in him not to jump over the table and plummet his fists into Tyrant's face. If it hadn't been for Mikayla and the girls, he would have, but he didn't want to alarm them, especially since Mikayla had no idea what was going on. Damian wasn't confident that she would choose him over her newfound lover. So instead, he clenched his fists and controlled his urges.

"Your time is almost running out," Tyrant reminded him. "I want my diamond."

"I'm looking for it."

"Not hard enough. My sources say you've been spending a lot of time in your mother's old apartment. Do you think she hid it there?"

"I don't think so," Damian said. "And if she did, shouldn't the goon you sent to kill her have found it? Why don't you just have one of them look for it? Why me?"

"Remember, Jewel's death was an accident. I never wanted to kill her, but sometimes things happen," Tyrant said like he couldn't care less. "And everyone knows that the debt of the deceased gets passed down to the children."

Damian took note of how he said the word *children*. His mind instantly went to his sister upstairs. He could faintly hear her giggling with Zuri, happy as could be.

"You leave her out of this," Damian barked.

"I'm afraid I can't do that," Tyrant said. "You see, if you fail, then I kill your son. What do I really get from that? Besides the satisfaction of seeing you break down, the answer is nothing. If my diamond is really lost to the world, then I think Mikayla is a fair exchange for that. That is, until I get tired of her."

"I'll kill you!" Damian lost his sense for a moment and jumped up from his seat.

"That wouldn't be wise, my friend. If something happens to me, nobody will be seeing the outside of this house ever again. And that goes for your little nieces. Sit."

Damian gritted his teeth and did as he was told. He was stuck between a rock and a hard place. There was only one thing that he could do to fix the trouble Jewel had caused.

"Find my fucking diamond," Tyrant sneered.

"I told you I'm working on it. Press me this hard in a month if I still don't have it," Damian said.

"One question though, Damian."

"What?"

"If you do find it, how can I trust that you won't just run off like your mother did?"

"Because I want to wash my hands of you completely," Damian answered honestly. "Now that I know what you look like, I never want to see you again."

"Good. I'm glad you think that way." Tyrant eyed Damian, trying to see if he was telling the truth. "But just in case, look at Mikayla as collateral and extra insurance if you do find it and try to keep it for yourself."

Damian opened his mouth to say something, but he heard footsteps coming their way.

Mikayla had come back down to rejoin them. The first thing she noticed was Damian's stony face, and he was sure she could feel the chill in the atmosphere. Her eyes darted from him to Tyrant as she tried to figure out what could have happened in her absence.

"What happened?" she asked and turned to shoot daggers with her eyes at Damian. "What did you say?"

"Everything is good, baby," Tyrant said, giving her a sweet smile and extending his hand to her. "Damian was just telling me what he would do to me if I hurt you."

"Was he, now?" Mikayla said, still glaring at her brother.

"Yes, he was. And I can't blame him." When Mikayla took his hand, he pulled her close so that she was standing directly in front of him. "I mean, look at you. You are stunning. If you were my sister, I would want to protect you by any means necessary."

The last few words he said were poised so innocently, but Damian knew the deadly threat behind them. Tyrant was serious. Damian could tell that he'd wooed his way into Mikayla's affections. It would be hard to prove to her that he wasn't the good detective that he made himself out to be. Not without any solid proof or without putting her in danger. However, for the moment, she was safe. Damian was confident that Tyrant wouldn't do anything to hurt Mikayla right then, and he decided that it was time for him to take his leave. He pushed away from the table and stood to his feet.

"Leaving already?" Tyrant, who was now acting like nice old Brandon again, said.

"I have a few things to handle," Damian said.

"Let me walk you to the door," Mikayla said and kissed Tyrant on the lips. "Brandon, I'll be right back, okay?"

She walked Damian to the door, and he was expecting her to go off on him. Instead, she gave him a hug at the door. He was shocked, to say the least. When she pulled away and looked up at him, he had second thoughts about leaving her there with Tyrant. As he looked in her eyes, he stopped seeing what she'd put him through, and instead saw what she'd gone through herself. She may have had more money than him, but her life hadn't been easy either. She'd gone through so much, and she didn't deserve any more heartache. But it was too late for that.

"I appreciate you for wanting to look out for me," she said, looking up at him.

"I just want to make sure you're on your *P*s and *Q*s. Not everything that's wrapped in a nice package is good for you," he told her.

"I know that. But I'm a big girl. I can handle myself."

"Can you?"

"Yes," Mikayla told him. "After Charles, I told myself I would never be in that position again. Brandon is a good guy, Damian. And maybe, if you stick around this time, you'll see that."

"Okay," was all he could think of to reply. "I'll talk to you later, Mikayla. Maybe we can set up a day where I can get the girls, if that's okay with you."

"They would like that," Mikayla told him and patted him on the arm. "Take it easy out there."

"No doubt."

With that, Damian left. As he walked to his car, he glance toward Mikayla's kitchen window. Tyrant was standing there, watching him. Damian felt the hairs on the back of his neck stand up. Something was telling him that Tyrant was enjoying the game he had forced Damian to play. Damian hoped that it would be over soon.

The night was still young, and he had time to go check out Winx. There was a reason Jewel made mention of it in her notepad. He just needed to figure out what that reason was.

Chapter 18

Mikayla

When Mikayla walked back into the kitchen, she was all smiles. Brandon was leaning with his backside on the counter and facing her. She had barely been able to keep her eyes off him the entire dinner. The way his shirt lay on his muscular frame was so sexy. The last person she'd been so physically attracted to was Tank, the singer. In her hand, she was carrying his plate, which had almost been licked clean. She placed it in the sink behind him and pressed her body against him.

"Well, it's safe to say that you enjoy my cooking," she said, looking up at him with a grin.

"Out of all the plates out there, you're going to single mine out," he joked.

"Yours *is* the only one that looks like you haven't eaten in a week!" she said and squealed because he began to tickle her. "Okay, okay! I give up!"

She pulled away from him and ran to the living room. He was right behind her. She couldn't outrun him, and when he caught her, they both fell in a fit of laughter onto the couch. When she looked up, his lips were close enough to press against hers, so she did. They shared a kiss full of desire, one that lit a fire in the pit of Mikayla's stomach. She hadn't been with another man since Charles, and until then, she hadn't desired to.

Brandon rubbed the outer part of her thighs, working her dress up, and Mikayla felt her legs slowly opening under him. His kisses went from her lips to her neck, and a small moan escaped her. The sides of her neck were among her favorite spots to get licked, and she felt tingles shooting down her body. Everything he was doing was sending a signal to her love spot and turning her on. If they didn't stop soon, he was going to have her butt naked on that couch with her daughters upstairs. But she wanted to so bad. Maybe he could just put it in real quick—

"No." Mikayla placed her hands on Brandon's chest and pushed him away. She quickly sat up and adjusted her dress while shaking her head. "I'm sorry. This isn't right. It isn't romantic, and I thought it would be romantic. My daughters are upstairs, and they're still awake. I just don—"

"Mikayla!" Brandon interrupted her and grabbed her hands to stop her from talking. "It's okay. We don't have to rush. I have a feeling that we will have more than enough time for all of that."

He smirked at her, but Mikayla was too busy taking a breath of fresh air to notice. She was happy that he wasn't upset with her.

The rest of the time he was there, they caught up on the news and watched a few shows before he left. When he was gone, she went upstairs to tuck Zuri and Kai in. Kai was already asleep, but Zuri was still up, messing around on her phone. Seeing her mother enter, she set it down and lay on her side.

"Hey, baby, did you finish your homework?" Mikayla asked, fluffing Zuri's pillow.

"Yes," Zuri answered. "Thank you for helping me."

"You're welcome. I want you to get some sleep and leave that phone alone, okay? I don't want to have to take it."

"All right. Mommy?"

"Hmm?"

"Is that detective your boyfriend?" Zuri had plopped her head on her hand and was staring intensely at Mikayla.

Mikayla felt a talk coming on, so she sat down on the edge of her daughter's bed and smoothed her hair back. She searched her own brain for an answer to the question. She didn't consider what she and Brandon had going on a serious relationship, but it definitely had the potential to become one.

"No, he's not my boyfriend. He's my friend," she finally answered.

"A friend who takes you out on dates?" Zuri inquired doubtfully.

"Yes, we're testing the waters right now, that's all."

"Well, what about Daddy?"

"What about your father, Zuri?"

"Aren't the two of you still married? Isn't it wrong if you date someone else?"

Mikayla sighed. "A lot of what your father did to me while in this marriage was wrong. In my heart, I am no longer bound to him. Soon I will not be legally bound to him anymore either. He wasn't someone I should have ended up with anyway."

"So you regret Kai and me?" Zuri's face dropped, and Mikayla instantly wished she would have made a better choice of words.

"Never in a million years, Zuri," Mikayla promised and rubbed her back. "You and your sister were the best things that ever happened to me. I just meant that the love between your father and me died a long time ago, and we should have left with it. But don't for one second think that just because we aren't together anymore means we love you guys any less."

"Are you sure?"

"Positive."

"All right," Zuri said, seeming satisfied with her mom's answer. "I don't think the detective is the one for you though, Mommy."

"And why not?"

"I don't know. I just don't like him. Uncle Damian doesn't like him either."

"Why do you say that?"

"I don't know. There's something about him I don't like. And I can tell Uncle Damian feels the same."

"Well, you and Uncle Damian just haven't given him a chance. You'll warm up to him," Mikayla said and kissed her on the forehead. "Now, go to sleep, little one. I'll see you in the morning." She got up and turned Zuri's light off before shutting her bedroom door.

After cleaning the dining room and kitchen, Mikayla made her final rounds around the house. She didn't plan on going to bed right away that night. Not only did she want to update her blog, but she wanted to enjoy her chocolate chip ice cream to herself.

With her laptop and cellphone in tow, Mikayla went inside her office. She flicked the switch and was instantly filled with so much warmth. It was her place of peace, and there was nothing that could disturb her energy when she was inside. The walls were white and beige, and there was golden décor hanging from them. She sat down at her white marble customized desk and opened her laptop.

She started working right away, naming the blog post "Why I Stayed." Writing for The Sisterhood had never been hard for her, because she spoke about her real experiences. She thought that was why other women connected with it the way they did. They felt the passion in her words. With her blog, Mikayla didn't want to teach sadness and shame. She wanted to show that no matter what horrors they faced in their pasts, they could have a future if they just let go of all toxicity.

She was so deep into her writing that she didn't hear her phone ring until it went off twice. She hurried to answer it without checking the caller ID.

"Hello?"

"I'm only going to offer this once. You can keep the house, and I will pay child support, but that's all you get."

"Charles?" Mikayla said, scrunching up her face at the sound of his voice. "It's almost midnight. Why are you calling me?"

"You heard me. You can get the house and child support."

"My lawyer said that I'm entitled to fifty percent of everything, so that's what I'm taking," Mikayla said into the phone. "She also said that if we go to court, with all of the evidence of abuse in the past and the affairs, I could walk away with all of it. So be happy I'm only taking half."

"Mikayla, I'm warning you. Don't do something you're going to regret. You know what I'll do to you."

"No, I know what you did to me. I'll kill you before I ever let you hurt me again. The next time you'll see me is when I'm signing those divorce papers and you're signing my check. After that, if it doesn't have anything to do with our children, stay the hell away from me."

She disconnected the phone and dropped it on her desk like it had burned her. She was breathing heavier than normal, and her heart was pounding. How dare he? He still spoke to her as if she were so small, as if she were nothing. Once the divorce was final, she had plans to put the house up for sale and move somewhere else. She wanted to rid herself of every bad memory she had that was attached to it. It was time to put him behind her.

He'd wound her up so much that she couldn't finish her blog right away. She opened a search bar and started looking at houses currently on the market. She wanted something that Kai and Zuri could grow up in and come back to if they ever needed. Somewhere that was homey even before any furniture was placed inside it.

Her nerves naturally calmed as she began envisioning the holiday season in a new place. There was one house that caught her eye. It was a five-bedroom, four-bathroom ranch style home. Three of the bedrooms were upstairs, and the other two were downstairs. It was beautiful, and it had everything from stainless steel appliances to the wood flooring that she loved so much. There was enough room for Damian if he ever wanted to come visit, or her friends if they ever wanted to stay at the house. When Mikayla saw the asking price, she thought it was a little pricey, but maybe if she made an offer she could talk them down. With the money she would be getting from Charles initially and every month on top of that *and* her own income, she would be able to afford it.

She felt herself growing excited. It had taken too long for her to be able to start living her life the way she wanted, and now she never wanted to stop.

Her phone ringing again interrupted her thoughts. She let out a frustrated sigh, sure that it was Charles again. This time, she checked to see who it was before answering. She felt relief when she saw the caller ID.

"Hey, Charlie girl," she said.

"Hey, Kay Kay," Charlie said, sounding as if she were wide awake. "I was hoping you'd still be up. Emerson's ass didn't answer my call."

"Jacob probably put her to sleep," Mikayla said with a giggle. "What's up, girl?"

"I was just calling to say I've given you ample time to tell me on your own."

"Tell you what?"

"Bitch, Emerson might have been able to fool me, but you can't. Everything about you all the way down to your Facebook statuses screams 'I got a man.' So spill it, who is he?"

"I don't know what you're talking about," Mikayla said, trying to keep a straight face just in case Charlie could hear her smile through the phone. "Everything has just been going well. I'm about to be a divorced and paid woman. The girls are doing well in school. Damian and I are working on our relationship. Things are just good right now."

"Blah, blah, blah. Get to the part about the man."

"Why do you think there is a man?" Mikayla giggled but was met with silence. She could see the blank expression on her friend's face in her head, and that only made her laugh harder. "Okay, okay. Maybe I am seeing somebody, but I'm not ready to bring him around yet. We're just testing the waters. And this is my first time dating after Charles, so I'm just trying to take things slow at first."

"So, you haven't gave him the booty then?"

"No, not yet."

"Girl, even if it doesn't go anywhere, I think you should go ahead and get you some dick. How long has it been? Too damn long!"

"I'm going to ask for you to not be clocking what I do with my pussy," Mikayla joked.

"I'm just saying. That motherfucka is probably like a dam waiting to be broken."

"I just want the time to be right, that's all. I don't want to rush it, because I actually like him. I've waited this long, so a little longer won't hurt."

"Well, don't make him wait too long."

"I know." Mikayla rolled her eyes. "Where's Mason at? Why are you up harassing your best friends?"

"He's not home yet, but he should be on his way now."

"How's everything been going with the two of you?"

"*Girrrl*," Charlie started, and the way she said it made Mikayla sit up straight in her seat, preparing to hear the tea. "Let me tell you about this whore detective at his job. *Detective Lawson*. Do you know this heffa made a pass at my man?"

"What?"

"At work!"

"Shut up! You lie!"

"Bitch, I'm dead serious. And I knew something was up by the way she looked at him. Like she just wanted to eat him up, girl. I should have beat her ass right then."

"So, how do you know that she made a pass at him?"

"He told me! If he wouldn't have handled it himself, your girl was going to be on the news for murder."

"I can't believe the nerve of some of these women," Mikayla said, truly shocked. She knew firsthand what it was like to have women all over her man. It wasn't a good feeling. "Did he fire her?"

"No, but she's on her last leg," Charlie said. "I trust my man, but it would make me a lot more comfortable if she was out of there."

"I know it would. But Mason is a good man. You can trust him," Mikayla told her. "So, ma'am, when is this grand opening so I can clear my schedule?"

"Girl, cleared schedule or not, your black ass better be there. You and Emerson. I'm going to have it the second to last week of January. Actually, that's the day before Kai's birthday now that I think about it. You're going to be partying all weekend."

"Apparently."

"Unh-uh, don't say it like that. My event is going to be one for the books. We're going to have a catwalk, food and drinks. Ahh! It's going to be so lit. I can't wait. I just can't believe it's all working. And now to have Mason behind me, it just all feels so right."

"Who would have thought that our ghetto asses would have grown up to be bosses?" Mikayla laughed. "I'm so happy for you, boo."

"Thank you." Charlie paused and got quiet for a moment. "Lord, I hear this child waking up. Let me go see what his deal is. If you talk to Eme before me, can you tell her when the event is? Tell her that it starts at five."

"Okay. I love you. Good night."

"Good night."

After she hung up, Mikayla had to admit that she had indeed gotten sleepy. But she still had work to do. She battled through her yawns and drooping eyes to finish her blog and post it live. When she got up to leave her office, she stopped at the doorway to look over her shoulder. She loved her writing sanctuary. A small smile found her lips before she switched off the light.

Chapter 19

Damian

When he first got to Winx, Damian had no idea what to expect. It was in a brick building on a street corner. There was nothing special about it, which was strange, because why wouldn't you want to have some bells and whistles to attract people to your club? There was no one outside but a single security guard watching the door. He was big, black, and his scowl seemed to be part of his outfit.

"If you don't have a membership, there is a three-hundred dollar cover," he said after he checked Damian's ID and patted him down.

"Three hundred dollars?" Damian asked incredulously. "For that much, Nicki Minaj *and* her booty better be up in there."

When the security guard gave him a blank stare, Damian sighed and pulled out the picture of Jewel from his wallet. He held it up to the guard's face, forcing him to look at it.

"I'm looking for this woman. Her name is Jewel," Damian told him. "She had the name and address of *this* club written down, and I'm just trying to figure out what she was doing here."

"Is she missing?"

"Something like that. She was murdered recently."

The security guard's eyes went wide. "Jewel is dead?"

"Yes, she is. You knew her?"

"I knew her briefly. She had just started coming here," he said and looked Damian up and down before opening the club's door. "I have someone who's gonna want to talk to you. Come with me."

The doorman walked inside the club, and Damian followed closely behind. "What's your name?" Damian asked.

"William."

They went through a few doors that were key card access only before they got to a large open room. Whatever Damian thought Winx was, he had been wrong on all counts. It was a club, all right, but not the kind where people danced, not even exotically. Soft melodies played in the background, and everyone around him wore a mask. The only thing he could see were their eyes. There were people of all shapes, sizes, and colors. Some were dressed, some were barely dressed, and others were flat out naked. Damian had done some freaky things in his life, but none as freaky as this place. To the right of him there was a young woman pulling anal beads from another woman's ass with her teeth, while another woman ate her pussy from behind her. Damian was wondering what his mother was doing in a club like this.

William led Damian to a door on the other side of the room, and they passed an orgy of three men and five women.

"Is this some sort of sex club or something?"

"Not as slow as you seem," William said sarcastically. "We're passing through the main room right now. Pretty much everything goes, but the gays tend to stick to the Red Room. They're into some pretty kinky shit, so they like to do their own thing. If you're into being dominated, we have the Black Room. This place is usually membership only, but A. J. will want to hear about what happened to Jewel."

"Why?"

"Ask A. J.," William said when they reached the door. He opened it and pointed Damian down a flight of stairs. "Once you're downstairs, it's the first door on the right."

Damian nodded his head once and headed down. He followed William's instructions and went to the first door on the right. There was a sliding door peephole that slid open the moment he knocked on it. A pair of cold eyes met his and sized him up.

"Who the fuck are you?" the voice of a woman said.

"I'm Damian."

"Well, Damian, what do you want?"

"I'm Jewel's son."

"Jewel's son?" The tone in her voice changed, and the coldness left her eyes. "How do I know you're telling the truth about who you are, boy?"

Damian once again pulled the photo from his wallet. The woman grunted when she was satisfied with the proof provided. She closed the peephole and began to unlock the door. Damian swore he heard no less than eight locks unlock before it swung open, revealing a woman who looked to be about his age. She was about five foot five and thicker than a Snicker. She wore her hair in a big afro, and the black leather dress she had on made her waist look smaller than it was.

Damian was welcomed inside of what seemed to be a large suite. There was a large screen television, a couch, a desk, and an adjoining room with a king-size bed. If Damian didn't know better, he would have thought he was in a hotel. His eyes fell on a few large mounds of money on the couch.

She noticed him looking and shrugged her shoulders. "Sex is the most lucrative business in the game," she said simply.

"Are you a sex trafficker?"

"No." She laughed at his nerve. "Nobody here is being forced to do anything. In fact, they pay to come back time and time again."

"Oh. Uh . . ." He cleared his throat. "I was looking for A. J."

"You're looking for A. J.?" She put a hand on her hip and cocked her head at him. "You're looking at her."

"You're A. J.?"

"That's what I said, ain't it?" she said, looking at him like he was stupid.

"Well, then you're the one I'm looking for," Damian said and pointed at the dining room table. "Can we sit down and talk?"

A. J. nodded her head and pulled a chair out for herself. He sat across from her and looked in her face. At first, he thought she was the same age as him. Now that he actually looked, he wasn't so sure. She had smooth skin, but the corners of her eyes were slightly wrinkled.

"Trying to figure out my age?" she asked, clearly amused. "Nosey, just like your mama. She sat in that very spot and stared at me for thirty minutes trying to figure that out. She guessed right, though. Said it was because she always had a knack for people. All *you* need to know, however, is that I am older than what you think."

"And how did you know Jewel?"

"We were lovers."

"What!" Damian almost choked on his air.

"We met when she first moved back here. She came as a plus one with one of my regulars. Sometimes I allow my members to do that. It helps keep business booming. We had our first encounter in the Main Room. She wasn't shy, and I liked that. I could tell she was fucked up inside. I liked that, too, because we were one in the same," A. J. said, smiling fondly. But quickly, her smile turned sad. "But that love affair was short lived."

"You know she's dead?"

A. J. nodded her head and blinked back her tears. She opened her mouth to talk, but shook her head because no words came out. On the table, there was a pack of cigarettes. She grabbed one, lit it, and took a long drag to calm her nerves.

"Yeah, I know she's dead," A. J. said almost tearfully. "She called me right before that bastard busted through her door. I spoke to her right before he killed her. The last thing she said to me was, 'Maybe we'll have a chance in another lifetime.' The next thing I know, she turns up dead."

"Did you know that Tyrant was after her when you first started—uh—dating?"

"Not at first, but eventually she told me. She didn't want me to get hurt by being wrapped up with her. When I asked her why she wouldn't just give the diamond back, she said that she wanted to leave her kids and grandkids something, and a million dollars was a good start. She'd found somebody to buy the diamond for just over that mark, but then she started to get jumpy. She told me she'd hidden the diamond in a safe place with someone she trusted."

"Who?" Damian asked

A.J. shrugged. "I don't know. All she ever said after that was she'll know when to open the box. I thought she was just getting paranoid, but she wasn't. I could have kept her safe." A. J. clenched her eyes shut to hold the tears back, but a few fell anyway.

"Why didn't you come to the burial if she meant so much to you?"

"I guess I just wasn't ready to say goodbye," A. J. said, sniffling.

"I wasn't either. And I still haven't had any real time to mourn, because I'm too busy trying to save what's left of my family. I have to figure out who Jewel left the diamond with. Unless you have a million dollars on hand?"

"I wish I could help you out, baby," she said sincerely. "I don't have that kind of money laying around."

"Then I have no choice. If her purpose in taking it was so that we can live, then my reason for giving it back is so that we can stay alive. So, please, if she said anything else, tell me." The tone of his voice was desperate.

"She didn't say anything else. I mean, she kept talking about butterballs, but that's it."

"Butterballs?"

"Butterballs," she confirmed.

"What does that mean? That she left it inside a turkey?"

"I don't know." A. J. stood up and walked over to one of the money mounds. She grabbed two big handfuls of hundred-dollar bills and brought them back over to Damian. "I might not be able to give you a million, but I can give you a little something to hold you over for a while."

"You don't have to do that."

"Yes, I do," she insisted. "I know the world hasn't been kind to you since you got out. I can't imagine the things you've had to do to make ends meet. So, you better take this money, boy. And don't make me tell you twice."

"Thank you," he said, taking the money. "For everything."

He rolled it into two bankrolls and stuck them into his pocket before standing up. A. J. nodded at him and lit another cigarette. He was almost to the door when her voice stopped him.

"Damian?"

"Yeah?"

"You be careful, all right?"

Damian nodded. *Easier said than done*, he thought.

Chapter 20

Charlie

"Ahhhh!"

Charlie's back arched as she let a high-pitched squeal loose through her lips. Her legs were up in the air, and Mason was between them, digging her out something vicious. Beads of sweat were falling from his forehead as he drilled her, and Charlie couldn't name a sexier sight. She opened her legs wider so that he could have even more access to her ooey-gooey center and at the same time clenched her teeth. His thick rod pounding her out hurt so good, and she didn't want him to stop. The wet sloshing sounds her pussy was making proved that.

Mason had turned her on so much the night before by making dinner, putting MJ down to bed, and running her a hot bath. If he kept that up, he would be waking up to pussy in his face every morning. They were on their third round before Mason had to leave for work, so Charlie was milking every second.

"This pussy feels like heaven, Charlie," Mason grunted, twisting up his face.

She knew what that look meant. His climax was just around the corner, and she wanted to make sure she met him at the finish line. Licking her fingers, she worked them around her clit and sent power jolts through her body.

"Mmm." She moaned as Mason continued to thump against her spot while she wound her fingers. "Mason. Mason. Mason!" She exploded, shooting her juices on his crotch and thighs.

He lowered his eyes and licked his lips at the sight. His breathing grew rigid, and he pumped a few more times before he came. He pulled out and shot his seed over her flat, bare stomach. While he stroked all of his nut out, Charlie played with her nipples for him. She watched his meat jump a few more times and one last glob of cum drop from the tip.

"Damn, girl." Mason let out a huge breath. "That pussy does it to me every time." He bent down and kissed each of her nipples before pressing his lips against hers.

Her tongue slipped inside of his mouth and intertwined with his. She felt her clit start to tingle again and started to move her hips, but Mason pulled away.

"Oh, no you don't." He wagged a finger at her.

"But, baby, I'm horny." She pouted.

"We just went three rounds," Mason said, looking at her with wide eyes. "Wasn't that enough for you?"

"Not when the dick is this good," she said and stroked his softening manhood. "Plus we have to make up for lost time."

Mason had stood firm on his promise to Charlie and had been home more. It made her happy to see his effort. Marriage was something that had been on her mind lately. She and Mason, of course, played with the idea, but they hadn't talked in great depth about it. With them being as distant as they were, Charlie had been having second thoughts about if she even wanted to be married at all. But now, with Mason acting like the man she fell in love with again, the thought of spending forever with him sounded appealing.

"I'll be sure I have some hot and ready for you when I get off," Mason said, moving her hand and heading for the closet. "What do you have planned today, anyways?"

"I'm going to the store today. I'm so ready for the opening, baby. It's going to be amazing," she told him.

"Is everything set up inside?" he asked from inside the closet.

She'd taken him to the store location the week prior, and at the time, there was stuff everywhere. He hadn't seen it all set up like it was now. She and a couple of hired hands had turned her dreams into reality. The only thing she was waiting on was one more dress line, but that would be there before the grand opening.

"It is now," she answered. "I can't wait for you to see it. I'm going to do a video announcement for the date of the grand opening, and both Eme and Kay Kay said they would repost it. Shivelle is also going to make her own announcement, so we're expecting this to be big."

"Words can't describe how proud of you I am, baby," Mason said, exiting the closet with his work suit in his arms. He stopped to look at her naked frame fondly. "You are the embodiment of a goddess, do you know that? You deserve everything you want out of life. And I'm happy that I'm still making that list."

"Aw, thank you, Mason," Charlie said, blinking back a few tears. "I just want to build something for our family."

"MJ is going to have a rich mama," he joked. "You gon' buy me a Maserati when you hit big?"

"Boy!" she exclaimed and threw a decorative pillow at him.

"All right, I'll settle for a Chevy truck," he said with a fake exasperated sigh and went to their master bathroom. "Hey, babe? I was thinking I might as well take MJ to daycare when I head over to work."

"Really?" Charlie raised an eyebrow because he'd never offered to drop him off before. "I thought you didn't approve of daycare."

"Two working parents have to do what we have to do." He shrugged. "Plus, I think the social interaction is doing him some good. I think it's time I saw the place that my son spends a lot of his time at. Maybe I'll sit and watch him play with the other kids for a little bit."

"Won't you be late to work?"

"Detective Lawson can handle things in the office for a little while."

"Oh." At the sound of her name, Charlie felt herself tense up. She got up from the bed without another word and wrapped her robe around her. She was about to leave so she could start getting MJ ready, but Mason grabbed her hand softly and made her look at him.

"Do you trust me?" he asked simply.

"Of course I trust you."

"You don't ever have anything to worry about with me. This is where I want to be. With you, MJ, and whatever gremlins come after him. I want you to be my wife."

From the jacket pocket of the black suit in his hands, Mason pulled out a small box. Placing the suit on a chair in their bedroom, Mason got down on one knee in front of Charlie.

She was frozen where she stood. It felt like the blood in her veins had stopped flowing. A chill swept through her body. When he opened the box and she saw the size of the diamond, her eyes almost popped out of their sockets.

Is this really happening? she thought to herself.

"This wasn't how I planned on doing this. I had a romantic candlelit dinner with rose petals all planned out, but there doesn't seem like a more perfect time than now," he said, looking into her tearful eyes. "I love you, Charlie Dixon, and I can't see myself living out my life with anyone but you. I want to get rid of your last name and replace it with mine. Will you marry me?"

"Y–yes," Charlie was able to get out. "Yes, I will marry you, Mason!"

He slid the ring on her finger and stood up to embrace her. She clung to him and sobbed in his shoulder. He was right; it was perfect. The affection surging through her was so powerful that she didn't want to let him go. When she pulled back, she kissed him and wiped her eyes.

"You are so wrong, you know that?" she said, admiring her ring. "Doing all this and not even gon' give me some more dick."

"That's what you want?" Mason asked devilishly and glanced at the time. "I guess I can spare twenty more minutes. Come here."

With that, Mason cupped her pussy and pulled her back to him. A moan came from her lips, and she clenched her walls tightly. In moments, he had her in the air with her legs wrapped around his waist, screaming his name.

Charlie was all smiles as she moved around Elegant. She had barely been able to keep her eyes off the rock on her finger. She couldn't believe she was engaged and couldn't wait to share the news with her friends.

Inside Elegant, she busied herself by arranging dresses on the racks before she made her grand opening invitation video. The storefront windows were covered with black curtains because she didn't want anyone to know what she had in store until the opening, but she knew that they would be blown away when they saw the store. Charlie had really outdone herself, and she was very pleased with the sign in the front. It was the silhouette of the trail of a ball gown, but the longest part of the trail spelled out the word *Elegant*.

Everything was perfect, from the new light fixtures to the flooring to the position of all the gown racks. Shivelle said she wanted to look into starting a fragrance line as well, but wanted to wait and see how Charlie did the first year. It made Charlie unbelievably happy to see everything had unfolded exactly how she had envisioned.

She set up her camera so she could make her video. Charlie planned to stand in front of a few of her gowns on the wall to give viewers a little taste. She pressed the record button and got in position.

"Hey, you guys! Charlie Dixon here, and I would love to cordially invite you to the grand opening of my new store, Elegant. Here at Elegant, we want you to feel wine-fine at any event you're at, and we have a little something for everyone. Come celebrate and shop with me. I hope to see you all there!" She held her smile at the end for a few moments.

She watched the playback and decided to do a few more takes. She got back in position, and just as she opened her mouth to speak, a bell chimed and someone entered the store. Charlie looked to the door. The newcomer was the last person Charlie would have ever expected to see there. She was wearing a peacoat over a black work suit, and her hair was in a long ponytail at the back of her head.

"Mason said that you were starting your own clothing line. And when he said you were here today, I had to come see for myself," Detective Lawson said, looking around. "Especially with the way he's been bragging on it. I have to admit, I'm impressed."

"Detective Lawson," Charlie said like there was poison on her tongue. "If this is your way of coming to apologize to me for your inappropriate behavior with Mason, you can save it."

"Oh, the contrary, actually," she said wickedly. "I'm actually here to see what it is he loves about you so much. Hmm."

Lawson started sizing Charlie up with her eyes, and Charlie braced herself. If she had to fight, she was going to be ready for it. She clenched her fists, and that didn't go unnoticed by Lawson, who just chuckled.

"Ready to fight for the man she loves," Lawson said, clicking her tongue on her teeth. "Cute. But you might as well give up while you can. I've spent countless of hours with Mason, and I can tell you now that I'm the perfect woman for him. Not you."

"You're an obsessed, crazy bitch!"

"No, I can assure you I'm very sane. I've just made the mistake of falling in love with a man who thinks he wants somebody else. But don't worry about it. That won't be a problem soon."

"You stay the hell away from Mason," Charlie warned.

"I would, but obviously he doesn't want me to. We still work together, don't we? He wants me. That's why he couldn't bring himself to fire me. I always get what I want. In the end, he will be mine."

"Oh, really? So why did he put a ring on *my* finger then?" Charlie asked, brandishing her new rock.

She could see how flustered Lawson was as she looked at Charlie's ring. Her lips moved as if she were talking, but no words came out. Charlie took pleasure in watching Lawson's face drop, even if it was only for a few moments.

"We're getting married, and there is nothing you can do about it." Charlie taunted her by blowing her a kiss. "Now, do me a favor and get the hell out of my store."

Detective Lawson took five steps and stopped when she and Charlie were nose to nose. The way she was look- ing at Charlie, a person would have thought she was the scum of the earth. Charlie stood her ground and shot the same cold stare back at her.

"Leave," Charlie repeated. "Before I call the police."

"You forget, I am the police," Lawson reminded her. She smirked one more time before she turned on her heels and left.

Charlie was so mad that she was shaking. She didn't even feel like making her video anymore. Whatever she had would have to work. She went to put the camera away and realized that it was still recording. She stopped it and played it back. Sure enough, she had caught the whole interaction with Detective Lawson on camera. Her voice was able to be heard clear as day, and she even stepped in front of the camera at one point.

"Yes, you are the police, but for how long?" Charlie said out loud.

The smile returned to her face and stayed there until she was able to show Mason the footage later that evening. He was stunned, to say the least. He left and didn't come home for another hour.

When he returned, he found her lying in bed with a book in her hands. He set the book aside and brought her fingers to his lips.

"Detective Lawson is no more. No one harasses my fiancée and gets away with it."

"She's fired?" Charlie asked hopefully.

"Yes. I made sure she boxed up her things myself," Mason said but looked troubled.

"Why are you looking like that? Are you sad that you had to fire her?" she asked and snatched her hands away.

"No, it's not that." He exhaled. "I'm just worried about you now, is all. I never thought Lawson's infatuation was really an obsession. I want you to carry a gun, Charlie."

"A gun?"

"A gun. It would give me peace of mind knowing that you're able to protect yourself."

"I don't think she's crazy enough to try anything else. She can't have you, and now she's lost her job. She'll get the picture and move on with her life."

She spoke with confidence, but Mason looked doubtfully at her.

"At this point, I don't know what she plans on doing. And the fact that she's a trained detective doesn't make me feel any better. Me firing her might have been the very push she needed to really do some crazy shit. I'd rather be prepared for nothing than not prepared and something happens. Keeping my family safe is my top priority. In the meantime, I'm going to put some cameras around the outside of the house, and I need you to invest in new locks at Elegant. We can go first thing in the morning to get your gun permit."

"Baby, I don't even know how to shoot a gun!" Charlie whined.

"I'll teach you," Mason said, kissing her tenderly on the lips. "You see what I do with the one on my body."

"I do." She giggled. "That's how we got our son.

"I hit that motherfucking target!"

"You sure did. But, baby, I don't remember how you did it. Will you show me?"

"You naughty girl," he said and kissed her again. "Before we do that, were you able to upload your invitation video?"

"Yes, I was. I just edited out all the craziness. It's almost at five thousand views, and I only posted it two hours ago. Mind you, that's on my page. When Emerson and Shivelle post it, I can't even imagine the type of attention it's going to get."

"It sounds like you could use some congratulations dick." He grinned seductively.

"No, I need some newly engaged dick. Come here."

Chapter 21

Emerson

"I would like to get to know if I could be . . . the kind of woman you can be down for."

Emerson moved around her kitchen, singing along to Brandy's voice. She was in good spirits, and wherever she went in the house, so did her Bluetooth speaker. She'd just finished sweeping and mopping and was about to start the dishes. The red kimono she wore draped from her body, and her hair was in one long braid that went down the middle of her head and stopped in the middle of her back. Her stylist had done the thing, and Emerson was especially glad, because she had a date with Jacob that evening.

She was swaying her hips to the music as she washed off a few plates. She was so into the music that she didn't hear anyone enter the kitchen. In fact, she didn't know she wasn't alone anymore until she felt someone touch her arm. She dropped the dish in her hands and jumped back.

"Ma!" she exclaimed when her head whipped around and saw who it was that had touched her. Her hand flew to her chest, and she took a deep breath. "You almost gave me a heart attack!"

"I'm sorry," Anna said and placed her bags on the counter. "But you know I have a key. You should expect me to just pop up from time to time."

"I thought you and Roger were across the state."

"He is, but I wanted to come check on the house and you. I'm here until tomorrow."

She began unloading, and Emerson saw that she'd brought over stuff to cook for breakfast—bacon, eggs, and pancake mix. Emerson looked at Anna like she was crazy and turned her music down.

"I can't eat that crap! That bacon looks like it's right off the pig's back."

"Oh, hush. I know your ass isn't a vegan, and that diet you're on has you looking like a bird. You need to eat something."

"Why can't you make me something like a fruit bowl and a bagel?" Emerson groaned.

"Because you eat enough of that. Now, move. I can finish cleaning in here while I cook." She bumped Emerson to the side with her hip and took over the kitchen. "How have you been feeling, baby? You never call anymore."

"That's because I want you to live and enjoy your life without always worrying about me," Emerson told her and took a seat at the island in the kitchen.

Over the last year, Anna had been traveling the world with her new man. So far, she'd been to Ghana, France, Greece, and Thailand. She'd never been able to explore the way she wanted to, because she was always so far up Emerson's butt. She never felt comfortable enough to leave Emerson for long periods of time, but over the past two years, she'd traveled because she was confident her daughter was getting better. Anna was dating a man named Roger, and they had moved in together. It was nice seeing Anna happy, but her worrisome ways hadn't gone anywhere.

"That's still no excuse to not call your mother." Anna pointed a spatula in Emerson's direction. "Even if it's not to tell me how you're doing, don't you want to know how I am?"

"I'm sorry, Ma. I've just been wrapped up in business and . . . other things." Emerson smiled as Jacob came to her mind.

"Mm-hmm. Well, those 'other things' better include Jesus himself, because that's the only excuse I'll accept for being neglected by my own child."

"Stop it." Emerson rolled her eyes. "Ain't nobody neglected you. Plus, you have Roger now. But to answer your question, I feel fine."

"That doctor you've been seeing still think it's a good idea to lower your dosage?" she inquired with an arched brow.

"Yes, she does." Emerson nodded. "I've been making significant strides, and I've gotten great at controlling my thoughts and emotions. She wants to learn more of a natural approach than drugging my body up."

"Natural approach?" Anna scoffed.

"Yes. Like breathing techniques, only surrounding myself with positivity, not bottling up my emotions. Being the real me at all times, and keeping things that make me happy close by. The key to a happy life is controlling the things around me. I try to limit the toxic energy in my life, and so far, it's been working. I haven't felt this good in forever."

"But for how long?" Anna asked with her hand on her hip. "Huh? How long is it going to last?"

"The doctor thinks that eventually I'll be off medication altogether. Or as needed. But for now, we are just taking baby steps."

"I don't think you should get off your medication, sweetheart. I mean, you said you were fine before, and look what you did to Charlie and—Oh, Emerson. I'm sorry. I didn't mean it like that."

She tried to catch herself, but it was too late. Emerson's whole demeanor changed after hearing her mother's words. She couldn't believe the lack of support she was getting. Her mouth was in a straight line when she spoke back to her mother.

"No, you said exactly what you meant. If I get off medication, I'm going to have another meltdown. Is that what you think?"

"Honey, I'm just saying be rational when it comes to making a decision like that. How do we know that it isn't the medicine you're on now that's making you feel so confident, huh? It would just put my mind at ease knowing you're still on your medication."

Emerson shot a mean look in her mother's direction and watched as she cracked the eggs and fried bacon that Emerson said she didn't want. Her heart was thumping, and she felt her emotions changing like the normal lights. She still had control, but she hadn't been on edge like that since—well, since the last time she saw Anna in October.

She and Roger were home for a weekend and had decided to have dinner with Emerson. Anna had done the same thing she was doing now, taking over and trying to limit Emerson's choices. Emerson hated it. Whenever Anna was around, she tried to make Emerson feel small. The last time they were together it went like, "Well, you know I've always had to do everything for you. Why do you think it's so difficult for you to keep a man?" Anna asked

"Mama, I'm doing fine. I've been on my own for a long time now."

"I know, but that condition of yours. Something just don't feel right."

Anna always reminded Emerson of her condition or tried to hint that she just *knew* something was off with Emerson even when she felt fine. She was toxic, and not only that; she was a trigger.

Now, Emerson had enough. She was confident in her own skin and knew she had control over herself. "Well, this isn't about your mind being at ease, is it, Ma? This is about me and me only," Emerson said slowly and evenly. "You know what? Get out."

"*Excuse* me? I'm still making breakfast."

"I said I didn't want any damn bacon or eggs, but here you are trying to force it down my throat. Get the hell out of my house." Emerson pointed her finger toward the kitchen exit. "You can keep your key, but I don't want you to come back until you're ready to breathe positivity in me. I'm starting to think the reason you like seeing me broken is because it gives you something to do and talk about. Not anymore. If you can't be on my side, that's when you can give me my key back. You won't be welcome here."

"I have done *nothing* but support you!"

"How, Ma? I just told you all the progress I've been making and spoke of *no* negatives, but you just had to shed your darkness, huh? You think supporting me is shoving pills down my throat to mask feelings. Well, the truth is that healing starts with pain. I had to feel all those feelings I was running away from, and guess what? I'm not running anymore!" Emerson jumped up and waved her arms around once. "I have a lucrative career, this big-ass house, and a man who loves me. *All* of me, even the crazy. So if *you* can't accept it, then you just weren't meant to. And I'm okay with that. Are you?"

Anna's eyes grew big as saucers. It wasn't the first time Emerson had raised her voice at her, but it was the first time she'd done so with her head held as high. She wasn't a completely new person, but she was well on her way to being one.

Anna made a "hmph" sound and snatched her wallet, food, and keys from the counter. She stormed out without saying another word to Emerson, who just shook her head. She got up so she could turn the burners off and threw the still runny eggs down the sink. After that, her appetite was gone, but she still grabbed a bagel from the fridge. She refused to let that exchange put a dent in her day. Maybe Anna would come around before she left, or maybe she wouldn't. Either way, Emerson would continue to live her life.

Dinner came too fast for Emerson. Even though Jacob had seen her a million times, she wanted to wear something that would make his eyes pop out of his head when he saw her. She tried on at least twenty outfits before finally settling on a long-sleeved satin dress with a deep cut at her cleavage that went down to just above her belly button. The dress stopped just above her knees and made her look more curvaceous than she thought she was. She had a professional makeup artist do a house call, and the braid in her hair set the whole look off.

When Jacob arrived to pick her up, his jaw dropped when she opened the door. His reaction was exactly the one she'd been going for. He didn't look too bad himself in his Tom Ford custom suit.

He took her to a nice steakhouse called Thompson's that she'd never been to before. They had amazing food and even better drinks. She and Jacob got lost in each other, and she put what had happened between her and Anna in the back of her mind. Emerson was so busy enjoying the moment that before she knew it, she was three glasses of wine in.

"Slow down, baby. I don't want to have to carry you to the car," Jacob joked from beside her and wiped his mouth with his cloth napkin.

"I'm just a little buzzed." She giggled and looked at him with low eyelids. "I really enjoy spending time with you. It's the best part of my day. I love you."

"I don't think I'll ever get tired of hearing those words come from your lips. There was a point in time that I thought I'd never hear them."

"I just didn't want to hurt or be hurt again," Emerson said honestly. "I thought that falling in love was something that I could control if I didn't give or take too much of anything. But you have proven to me that when it's meant to be, it's inevitable."

"So we were inevitable?" Jacob asked with a smart-aleck smirk.

"Boy, don't patronize me," she said, swatting his arm playfully. "I'm not saying I'm ready to walk down the aisle again any time soon, but I don't want you to go anywhere."

"And I don't want you to go anywhere, especially when you look as fine as you do tonight." His hand slid across her stomach and stopped at her hip as he leaned in for a kiss.

His lips tasted sweet like the wine they were drinking and were so soft against hers. Things were more perfect than she ever thought they could be. After she got Cali what she asked for, she also wrote her a check for five thousand dollars for signing an NDA. With that in her past, she was confident that no other skeletons would jump out of the closet on her. She could finally live and enjoy her life to the fullest.

She moaned softly into Jacob's mouth and thought to herself that it was time to leave or else the other guests were going to get a show. A throat loudly clearing was what broke their kiss. At first Emerson thought it was their server coming back to check on them, but the pretty woman standing beside their table wasn't dressed like the help. In fact, she was wearing a long-sleeved black Oscar de la Renta dress. Emerson had the same one.

She smiled at the woman, but the woman didn't pay her any mind. She was focusing her icy glare on Jacob. He gave Emerson a dumbfounded look, but that made her more confused than she already was.

"Hello, Jacob," the woman said, her voice matching her expression. "Funny to run into you here. And who is this?" The woman pointed at Emerson and rolled her neck.

Emerson raised her eyebrows and looked at Jacob, who seemed to be at a loss for words.

"Jacob, what's going on?" she asked. "Who is this woman?"

When Jacob still failed to find his voice, the woman flashed her hand at Emerson, whose eyes fell to the big rock on her ring finger.

"I'm Jayda, his wife," the woman said smugly. "Oh, silly me. He probably didn't tell you about me, did he?"

"W—wife?" Emerson stammered.

"Married for four years," Jayda said and turned back to Jacob. "So, this is what you've been up to?"

"Jayda, what are you doing here?" Jacob asked.

"No, the real question is, what are you doing here with this woman? Is this why you haven't been returning any of my calls?"

"What?" Jacob scrunched his face up like he had no clue what she was talking about.

Emerson couldn't breathe. It felt like the walls in the restaurant were closing in on her and she had to get out of there. She grabbed her clutch and tried to leave, but Jacob stopped her.

"Eme, please," he said, trying to get a hold of her arm.

"Get the hell off me." She snatched away with tears in her eyes. "Talk to your wife."

She ran out of the restaurant, not caring that she wasn't the one who drove. She would call one of her girls to come and get her, and if that failed, Uber. Emerson just needed to be as far away from Jacob as she could be. Every fiber of her being wanted to break down in tears, but there were too many people outside, and someone was bound to recognize her.

Married? Okay, maybe the situation with Cali might have been a little much, but she hadn't been hiding a whole spouse. And speaking of Cali, how could she not tell her that Jacob was married? The entire family had betrayed her. He told her he loved her, that he didn't want to be with anybody else, yet the whole time, he belonged to somebody else. It was too much.

Emerson's vision was blurry as she scrambled to find Mikayla's contact, and she had a sob caught in her throat.

"Emerson! Please let me explain."

She turned around to see Jacob bursting through the restaurant doors. The concern dripping from his face as he ran her way made her angry. He tried to wrap his arms around her, but she shoved him hard.

"I can't believe you!" she said to him. "You did all of this. For what? To embarrass me? This must be a restaurant you take her to for her to be able to find you."

"She was here with some friends. I had no idea she was going to be here, or else I wouldn't have come."

"Oh my God," Emerson groaned. "I've been running around with a married man. The blogs are going to have a field day with this one."

"Emerson, please—"

"No! You made me fall in love with you when I wasn't even ready to open up in this way to someone. All for me to find out you're married? To that bitch? You better get the hell out of my face before I grab this blade from my clutch and cut your ass!"

"Emerson, please don't cut me," Jacob said, putting his hands up to show he meant no harm. "I just want to explain myself. Please. I owe you that much. And then, when you're done listening to what I have to say, you can leave me alone if you want to."

Emerson felt like a helpless child. She didn't want to hear what he had to say, because she had already been cut too deep. But the only thing that could heal her wound was the cause of it. She was silent as she blinked her tears away, and Jacob used that as his window of opportunity.

"I apologize for not telling you about some details in my life, but I just wanted to start something fresh and new. I didn't plan on falling in love with you. It just happened."

"How could you feel comfortable starting something fresh with me if you're still married to somebody else?"

"*Was* married."

"What?"

"I was married, but not anymore. We were young and impulsive when we got married, and it took me a while to see her gold-digging ways. She never loved me, only my bank statement. I filed for divorce because that kind of life gets boring. A life with no love? No passion? Who wants to live like that? When I filed for divorce, we separated, and I wasn't going to let a piece of paper stop me from living my life, so I started dating. Jayda made it her business to sabotage any potential relationship I might have had. And when the divorce finalized five months ago, she left with all she came with—nothing. Well, except for the two hundred thousand wedding ring I bought her.

"I know it sounds bad, but when the divorce was final, I didn't feel the need to bring her up. I didn't want to worry you, especially when Jayda is nothing but a past mistake filled with toxic energy. That page has turned."

Emerson studied his face, and she could tell that he was telling the truth. She felt in her spirit that Jacob really loved her, and although she wanted to be angry, she had her own transgressions and made the decision to pick her battles wisely. She fell into his arms and let him kiss and comfort her.

"I would never do anything to break your heart," he whispered. "Never."

"I know," she told him.

A thought suddenly overcame her, and she pulled back from him with arched brows. "So, that's *your* ring? She still in there? Let's go get it."

She was already headed back toward the restaurant before she was done talking. She skipped the line, and once inside, she scanned the whole place until she found Jayda, laughing hysterically with a group of women, probably at Emerson's expense.

"If I go to jail, make sure you're my lawyer," Emerson told Jacob.

Before he could stop her, she took off toward Jayda's table. Jayda might have had a pretty exterior, but her core was rotten. She was going to learn that Emerson was the last person to play with.

"I still can't believe I made that bitch run out of here like that. Oh my God, poor thing. But that's her fault for choosing to sleep with my ex-husband," she was saying to her friends.

"Why are you still messing with that man?" one of her friends said, laughing.

"Because he took everything from me in the divorce, so until I'm satisfied with his level of misery, I'm going to make his life a living hell every chance I get."

"Well, I guess you got the right one this time." Emerson's voice caught them all by surprise. "You should be ashamed of yourself."

"Ashamed of what?" Jayda snapped out of her shock quickly. "Girl, trust me, I'm doing you a favor. You don't want Jacob."

"It sure seems like you do, though. Well, not him. You want his money, don't you? I used to be a broke bitch like you. The difference is I was my own come-up. I didn't need to use a man to get where I wanted to be."

"*Excuse* me?" Jayda stood to her feet and faced Emerson.

"You heard me. Now, you were ordered to give that ring back, so you have two choices tonight. Give me the ring, or get your ass beat by me, and I take the ring. Your choice."

The table next to them was tuned into them like their favorite TV show. One of the women recognized Emerson and gasped. She tapped the person next to her and pointed before speaking loudly.

"Isn't that Emerson Dayle? Didn't she, like, kill her best friend and get away with it?"

"No," her friend said. "She didn't kill her, but she almost did."

Just like Emerson heard them, Jayda did too. She gave Emerson a frightened look, and Emerson returned it with a wink. Jayda hurried to remove the diamond from her finger and almost flung it to Emerson.

"Good decision," Emerson said and turned on her heels, ignoring the looks she was getting throughout the restaurant.

When she got back to where Jacob was standing by the door, she gave him the ring. "Here. Sell it and buy me something nice. But let's get out of here before they call the police."

Chapter 22

Damian

Damian had found someone to take on the rest of Jewel's lease. He had put her things in storage and started staying in places that accepted cash as payment, like the motel he was in. He wanted to stay as off the map as possible.

He was in the middle of packing his duffle bag when there was a knock at the door. Pulling out his gun, he walked slowly to the door. Right before he got to it, a piece of paper was slipped forcefully under the door. It hit his shoe. He looked down at it then hurried to open the door. No one was there. He rushed outside, waving his gun.

"Ahhh!" A plump Hispanic housekeeper was coming out of a room next to his. She dove behind her cart when Damian turned her way. But other than her, there was nobody there.

He let his arm drop to his side and looked back at the paper that was still on the ground. He went back into the room and picked it up.

"Six days," he read out loud.

It was a reminder from Tyrant. So much for staying off the radar. Tyrant seemed to have no trouble finding him no matter where he was at. Crumpling the paper up, he tossed it to the side and tucked the gun away. He grabbed his belongings and left in a hurry.

The note was only one of the reasons he left. He also had promised Mikayla that he would pick up the girls. They didn't have school that Monday, and she needed to get some work done, so he offered to take them. Since he didn't have access to Braxton, he wanted to at least spend some time with them just in case things didn't go as planned.

He'd been searching high and low for a clue as to who Jewel would have trusted a million-dollar diamond with. It felt like he had come so far only to have hit a brick wall in the end. He thought maybe he could try to meet back up with Oddie in the coming days. Maybe Oddie knew more than what she had let on. So far, she was proving difficult to get in contact with, but that was all he had, so he'd have to keep trying.

It was just before noon when he pulled into Mikayla's driveway, and he had barely put the car in park when Kai and Zuri came running out of the house, bundled in their coats and scarves. Zuri got in the front seat, and Kai sat behind her.

"Hi, Uncle Damian!" Kai greeted him with a smile.

"Hey, Kai."

"I'm so glad you came when you did. She's crazy!" Zuri said through a fake smile. She waved back to Mikayla, who was standing in the doorway, waving at them.

He wasn't in the mood to laugh, but Zuri made him chuckle a bit. He pulled away from the house and drove off toward the end of the block.

"So, where to, ladies?"

"Ice cream!" they yelled in unison.

"Have you even eaten lunch yet? I don't think your mom would like that too much."

"I thought you were a cool uncle." Kai pouted in the back seat with her arms crossed.

"Why can't I be a cool uncle that respects your mom's wishes?"

"Because that's lame!" Zuri exclaimed.

"Lamer than lame!" Kai cosigned. "You'd probably get the worst uncle award for that."

"Now there's a worst uncle award." Damian faked disappointment. "I guess the only way to make sure I don't get that is to take you to get ice cream!"

"Yeah!" they shouted in unison.

It was amazing how the smallest things meant the world to others. As he drove, he glanced in the rearview mirror at Kai and caught her staring out the window with a frown on her face. The energy she'd just had a second ago was gone, and she seemed sad.

"You good back there?" he asked.

"I guess so," she said with a sigh. "It's just that I wish Grandma could be here for my birthday this weekend. I only got to have her for a short time."

"Yeah, me too," Damian told her. "I'm sure she would have loved to be at your party."

"I know if she could have been, she would have been. I was her Butterball."

Damian stepped on the brakes so abruptly that the girls flew forward. Their seat belts caught them and threw them back into their seats. He pulled over to the side of the road and turned to face Kai.

"What did you just say?"

"You could have killed us!" Zuri shouted from the passenger seat.

"But you didn't die," Damian told her and focused back on Kai. "Repeat to me what you just said, Kai. You were her what?"

"She called me Butterball, because my tummy pokes out a little. She said I would grow out of it like Mommy did," Kai said, giving him a weird look. "Are you okay, Uncle Damian? You're scaring me."

"Did Jewel give you anything?"

"Yes," Kai said, nodding her head. "A little box, but she said it was my present, and that I couldn't open it until my birthday. So I gave it to Mommy to hide until then. I told her it was from one of my classmates."

"Where did she hide it?" Damian asked, feeling his excitement level go up.

"I don't know. She promised not to tell me or anybody else until my birthday," Kai told him.

"Kai, listen to me. I need you to find out where that box is. It's important."

"Nope." Kai shrugged, not knowing how important what he was asking for was. "I'm not breaking my promise to Grandma. You'll get to see what it is when I see what it is. This Sunday, my birthday!"

"This Sunday?" Damian asked and did the calculations in his head.

Saturday was the day he was supposed to have the diamond to Tyrant. He was almost positive that Jewel had left the diamond to Kai. It all added up. He could tell his niece wasn't budging, and he was sure Mikayla wouldn't tell *him* where the gift was. Not without asking questions.

"She probably hid it in her office," Zuri spoke up. "She hides everything there because she thinks we don't know where the key to her desk is."

"Hey! I don't know where the key is!" Kai exclaimed.

"Hey, it's not my fault you've never thought to look under her pen cup." Zuri shrugged.

Damian let them bicker back and forth while he put the car back in drive and got on the road. The diamond had been at Mikayla's house the whole time—the last place that anyone would have ever thought to look. Jewel was cunning.

Now all Damian needed to do was figure out how he would get the diamond. It would have to be when Mikayla was gone, but he had no idea when he could pull that off without her knowing. He'd have to find someone who had access to the house outside of the girls and his sister. Someone who used to live there. Someone who had given him their card the last time Damian was face to face with him. Charles. Damian was sure Mikayla had changed the main locks on the house, but the side door that led into the basement looked like it hadn't had its locks changed in years. He wouldn't have put it past Charles to have a copy of the key.

His mind was reeling all the way until they reached the ice cream shop, and then finally, like magic, a light bulb went off in his head.

Chapter 23

Mikayla

Charlie's grand opening went off without a hitch. She looked beautiful rocking a pale pink dress from one of her own collections. She looked nothing short of elegant, not to mention she was floating around her new store flossing a new rock on her finger. At first Mikayla was worried about how Emerson would feel about it, but she was so wrapped up in Jacob that she didn't care.

"I guess it's time to really change my last name, huh?" she'd joked.

So many people turned up that there was a line to get in. Brandon was supposed to come as her date, but he said something had come up last minute. She was a little upset about it but figured they could catch up another time.

Mikayla thought they had just come to the opening to partake in the festivities, but there were so many people that actually came to shop, Charlie ended up short-handed. Mikayla and Emerson didn't hesitate to jump in and help out. Mikayla didn't know the first thing about measurements, but she could sure tell a woman what she did and didn't look good in. By the end of the opening, Charlie had made thirty thousand dollars in profit.

"Here," she said when she found them after everyone had gone home.

Mikayla and Emerson were hanging back at one of the tables with Mason and Jacob. Charlie tried to hand her friends some money, but they both looked at her like she was crazy.

"What's that for?" Mikayla asked.

"For coming in and saving the day!" Charlie said like it was obvious. "If it weren't for you guys, I don't think I would have made it tonight."

"Well, you did, and that's what friends are for." Mikayla pushed Charlie's hands back.

"Yeah, girl, I know you better get that money out of my face," Emerson told her, waving her hand once.

Charlie smacked her lips.

"You guys are aggravating."

"You need all your money anyways. Don't you have a wedding to plan?"

"Yes, I do!" Charlie squealed. "Oh my God, I'm getting married!"

Mikayla and Emerson stood up and jumped up and down with Charlie, squealing like little schoolgirls. There was nothing but happiness in the air that night.

Behind them, the men stood up, waiting for their women so they could leave.

"I'm gonna stay a little while longer, baby," Charlie told Mason.

"And I'll stay with her so I can take her home," Mikayla chimed in.

"I'll stay too," Emerson told them and then looked at Jacob. "Do you mind?"

"Nah, you and your girls do your thing. I'll stay up for you. Don't stay out too late. Remember, we have a crazy party to go to," Jacob said and winked at Mikayla.

"Oh, yeah," Mikayla said sarcastically. "We're going to so totally get chocolate wasted."

They all shared a laugh before the men left. The store was a complete mess, and Charlie's employees had gone home for the night already. It took almost an hour, but the three of them had Elegant looking spick-and-span by the time they were done.

Mikayla stood back and looked on in awe. "Damn, girl," she said. "You have a store."

"And I'm getting married," Charlie added.

"Miracles do happen!"

They giggled.

"When your divorce is finally final next week, we will all have our happily ever after." Emerson sighed in bliss.

"Okay, let me lock up and we can head out," Charlie said. "Kay Kay, did you park far? Because you know I don't like walking far in heels."

"Girl, you know I parked close. I don't even play those types of games in the cold!"

Charlie turned the lights off, and they stepped outside. They waited for her to lock up before embarking on the short journey to Mikayla's car. When they got there, Mikayla unlocked the doors, but before they got in, a crunching sound caught her attention. She was parked near a dumpster, and from behind it, someone wrapped in a blanket came limping toward them. They were hunched over, so she couldn't see their face. She guessed they were homeless by the filthy condition of the blanket.

"Can we help you? Sir? Ma'am?"

"Charlie!" Emerson exclaimed. "That is rude."

"What? I can't tell what they are with that blanket wrapped around them."

The person didn't say a word, and the girls huddled around Mikayla. The person in the blankets was making a sound like they couldn't breathe. But the closer they got, Mikayla heard that it wasn't a wheeze. They were saying a word over and over.

Katt

"What?" she asked.

"Mikayla. Mikayla. Mikayla."

"H—how do you know her name?" Emerson asked, forcing them all to take a step back.

"Mikayla. Mikayla. Mikayla."

"Freak! Come on, you guys. Let's go," Charlie said.

"I can't let you do that," the person under the blankets said quickly and pounced on them.

The last thing Mikayla remembered was a cloth going over her nose, difficulty breathing, and then darkness.

Chapter 24

Damian

"Where is it?"

"W—what?" Mikayla asked between sobs.

"You know exactly what I'm talking about. You thought I wasn't going to find out? Now, you have a chance to save your friends. Tell me what you did with it. You have five seconds."

Mikayla's eyes were on the gun Damian now had pointed at her friend's chest as he counted down. Her lips opened and closed like she wanted to say something, but she couldn't get it out. Charlie and Emerson were crying loudly, but that was just background noise to Mikayla.

"One," Damian said.

"No!" Mikayla screamed.

But he didn't care. That time, Damian didn't hesitate to pull the trigger. The gun went off loudly in his hand, and everyone, including Charles, jumped. At the last second, Damian had jerked his arm and shot the bullet into the ground. Emerson was visibly shaken, and Mikayla stared at him with horror in her eyes.

"I let you around my children," she spoke tearfully. "And this is how you're going to do me?"

"It's life." Damian shrugged his shoulders.

"Enough of this. I want this bitch dead!" Charles exclaimed.

He caught Damian off guard by snatching the gun from his hand and aiming it at Mikayla. His finger was already on the trigger before Damian could make a move to stop him.

Boom!

The shot rang out, and Damian's eyes went straight to Mikayla in terror. However, she was still alive and in one piece. He followed her gaze back to Charles and saw a stunned expression plastered on his face. He tried to speak, but his words came out as gurgles. Damian then took notice of the neat hole in his neck and the blood pouring from it.

Charles began choking on his own blood and dropped to the floor. He jerked a few times before finally, he was still. Damian's eyes went to the far back of the basement, behind where the women were tied up, and he saw someone come from the shadows.

"Tyrant," Damian said. "You were supposed to come when I got the diamond."

Tyrant, who was dressed in another suit, shrugged his shoulders.

"Sometimes I like to arrive to the party early," he said.

Tyrant came from the back of the basement and stood next to Charles's dead body with his gun still out. He looked down at Mikayla with pity in his eyes. When she saw him standing there, her gaze went from him to Damian, and back to him.

"B–Brandon?" she stammered. "But why?"

"Maybe because I'm not really a detective," Tyrant told her and then made a face. "I guess now would be a good time to tell you that my name isn't Brandon either."

"He's the man who killed Mama," Damian answered. "Because she stole from him. A diamond worth a lot of money."

"And your kind brother here has been looking for it for me."

"You're working with the man who killed your mother?" she asked disgustedly.

"What's it to you? You never gave a shit about us anyway," Damian said harshly.

"I thought we were getting better, though. I thought—I mean, you and the girls." Mikayla choked up.

"I just wanted to gain your trust so that we could find the diamond. It's in this house."

"I don't know where any diamond is! She didn't give it to me."

"Of course she didn't. Why would she? From what you told me, you two hated each other," Tyrant told her.

"She gave it to Kai," Damian told her. "She told her she couldn't open it until her birthday, and—"

"She gave it to me to hide," Mikayla remembered.

"Where is it?" Tyrant asked.

"U—upstairs. In my office. I—it's inside the first drawer in my desk. The key is under a big cup of pens."

Tyrant waved his gun at Damian and told him to go upstairs and bring the box to him.

"No funny business either. Need I remind you what happens if I don't get the diamond?"

Damian nodded his head and went upstairs to get the box. He was gone for only a few minutes, but when he came back downstairs, he had a small box wrapped in pink paper in his hands.

Tyrant couldn't hide his excitement when he snatched it into his own clutches. "Finally, you are mine again," he said as he ripped the paper and threw it to the side.

As he opened the box, his eyes and smile got bigger and bigger, until it was all the way open. The smile dropped instantly from his face as he stared at the contents inside. From it, he pulled out a small charm bracelet meant for a young girl. He held it up to Damian with a look of fury on his face.

"What the fuck is this, Damian? This doesn't look like my pink diamond!"

"Oh, I'm sorry. That's my bad," Damian said and pulled the diamond from his pocket. "Are you looking for this?"

The look on Tyrant's face was just like the diamond, priceless. It had been hard for Damian to stay in character, especially seeing Mikayla look at him like that. It was the same way she looked at him when he'd first gotten out of prison—like murk in clean water. But he had no choice.

Charles had given Damian the key under the pretenses that he would kill Mikayla when she got home that night and stage it to look like a burglary gone wrong. He wasn't supposed to die. Damian was just going to blackmail him and say that he would tell the police Charles hired him to murder Mikayla.

Damian had a feeling when he told Tyrant to meet him at Mikayla's house that he would find some way to sneak inside early. That was why he made Charles give him the key to the side door the day before. Damian snuck in when Mikayla was out grocery shopping and swapped the diamond for the bracelet.

"Give it to me."

"You know, at first I was really going to hand it over," Damian told him honestly. "But now, I'm not so sure."

"Think about your son, Damian," Tyrant warned, holding a hand out. "Give me the diamond. I'm not leaving without it."

"Nah, I don't think I will," Damian said, putting the diamond back in his pocket. "The only reason you've had me on strings for this long is because you threatened my family. It took me up until a little while ago to realize that you were never going to spare my family. We've seen your face, and something says that we won't live to tell a soul who Tyrant really is."

"Smart man." Tyrant chuckled. "The truth is, none of you were ever going to make it out alive." He raised his gun fast and started shooting at Damian.

The women screamed as Damian jumped out of the way and toward the gun Charles had dropped. He grabbed it, turned to Tyrant, and fired twice. Both of his bullets caught Tyrant in his chest, but Tyrant's bullet also struck him.

Damian felt fire in his right shoulder, but he watched triumphantly as Tyrant went down.

"Damian!" Mikayla cried out.

He struggled to his feet and went to where she was. He undid the ties on her hands with his good hand, and she took care of the ones on her ankles. She untied her friends, who were still shaking after witnessing two shootings.

Damian was losing blood fast and felt himself growing lightheaded. He fell back down, not able to keep his balance. Charlie took one look at all of the blood on his shirt and knew it meant bad business.

"I'm going to go start the car," she said. "Emerson, call the hospital and tell them to expect us. Mikayla, can you wrap his wound?"

"Yes. Here," Mikayla said, rushing over to him. She removed the cardigan she had on and tied it around his shoulder. "We need to get you to a hospital."

"I'm sorry about all this," he said weakly. "I couldn't tell you. He said he would hurt you and my son if I didn't get the diamond back."

"That's why you stayed in Baltimore after Jewel's burial," Mikayla said, and he nodded. "You could have told me what was going on, Damian. You didn't have to kidnap us."

"I didn't plan on grabbing your girls. I wasn't expecting all of you to ride together. And I didn't tell you what was going on because I didn't think you would believe me about Tyrant."

"I guess you have a point there." Mikayla exhaled. "I'm so stupid. I was so entranced by him. I didn't even care that he wasn't giving me updates about the case anymore. I should have known something was phony about him. I guess it was just nice to have someone's attention. I'm so *dumb*."

"Not dumb. They both did a number on you," Damian said, pointing at the bodies of Charles and Tyrant. "It wasn't your fault. Charles was a piece of shit. I almost killed him myself a few times when he thought I was really going to kill you. He wanted me to make it seem like a burglary gone wrong."

"That bastard. I know I'm for sure selling this house after this," she said, looking like she wanted to throw up. "And what kind of name is Tyrant anyway?"

Damian tried to laugh, but a searing pain shot across his chest, causing him to grimace.

"What are we going to tell the police?" he asked her. "I can't go back to prison."

"And you won't. We're going to tell them that my husband and the man he hired to kill me got into a terrible fight before the deed was done, and my husband was killed. Then you stopped by, saw what was going on, and saved the day. You'll be a hero," Mikayla told him.

"Do you think they're going to believe it?"

"They're not going to have a choice. And I'll make sure my friends corroborate our story."

"Thank you," he said, and she cupped his cheek.

"No, thank you. Now, let's get you up these stairs."

She helped him stand to his feet and walk to the stairs. He leaned on her as they went up. With the pain coursing through his body, he remembered something that lifted his spirits—the diamond in his back pocket.

"You know, a million is a lot of money," Damian told her. "Jewel wanted us to have it. What do you say we split it?"

"No." Mikayla shook her head. "With Charles dead, I'll be getting more than enough money. Not to mention the insurance policy *I* had on him. You keep it. Start over. Maybe one day I'll get to meet my nephew. Speaking of which, I can't believe I didn't know he existed!"

"One day soon," Damian told her as they stepped out the side door of the house. "Maybe I'll bring him here, provided I survive this gunshot wound."

"You better, or else I won't hear the end of it from the girls. Speaking of which, I've been meaning to kick your ass for letting them eat ice cream for lunch on Monday."

That time when Damian laughed, he accepted the pain.

They walked around to the front of the driveway, where Charlie and Emerson were waiting inside Mikayla's car. She got in the back seat with him to make sure he kept pressure applied to his wound.

"Mason is on his way to the hospital to meet us. He wants to get a sworn statement from Damian."

"Why?"

"I mentioned the guy's name, Tyrant, and that he admitted to killing Jewel. Mason went crazy. Apparently he's some psycho who goes around killing people for not paying their debts. His death and identity is going to be headline news tomorrow."

"Did you tell him anything else?" Mikayla asked nervously.

"Hell no. I'm not dumb. You haven't even told me what happened back there because I just *know* I can't tell them what my eyes saw."

"Good," Mikayla said, relieved, and in her next breath, she explained what the story would be.

"Got it," Charlie said.

230   Katt

"Got it," Emerson echoed.

"Thank you," Damian told them. "And Emerson, I'm sorry for hitting you. I just had to make it believable. I figured we were being watched."

"Yeah, yeah, yeah," Emerson told him. "Next time, just keep me out of your brilliant plans."

"You got it."

Epilogue

One year later

"Baby, all I want for Christmas, is youuuu!"

Emerson sang into a remote control like a microphone loudly in her fiancé's ear. They were sitting together in the living room, and she was perched comfortably on his lap. He made a face as if she had shattered his ear drum, and she hit him playfully.

"Unh-uh, don't be torturing that poor man like that!" Charlie said, entering the living room, carrying a plate for Mason.

"For real, I feel sorry for that man," Mikayla said, entering close behind Charlie.

It was Christmas day, and Mikayla couldn't think of a better way to break in her new home than by celebrating with her loved ones. The three of them had decided to share the holiday together with their families. Everyone was in footie pajamas and eating good. Damian had even popped up with Braxton and his ex-stripper girlfriend. He told Mikayla that they'd decided to try to work it out.

"I'm proud of you," she told him. She was worried that after he sold the diamond, he would just blow through the money, but he surprised her by investing in stocks and opening a few barbershops. The kids were upstairs out of the way of grownups, and the grownups were in the living room, acting like kids.

"I think the person she's torturing is right here," Jacob said and placed a hand on Emerson's growing baby bump. "He's probably in there turning flips."

"*She* probably thinks her mommy has the most fantastic voice," Emerson corrected him.

"Mm-hmm."

Emerson's pregnancy news came right after Charlie and Mason's wedding. It was a shock to her, especially since she wasn't trying. She honestly didn't think she could get pregnant, but there she was carrying a healthy bundle of joy. She couldn't wait until May so she could kiss her baby's cute little toes. Everyone was excited for her. Mikayla came with her to any doctor appointment Jacob couldn't, and Charlie had already designed the dress for her baby shower.

Her mother, Anna, had come to her senses and stopped treating Emerson like a fragile doll. She'd even stopped traveling so much so she could be there for Emerson as much as possible in her time of need.

Being as happy as she was proved to be hard at first because she wasn't used to life without drama. Slowly but surely, she grew accustomed to her stable life with Jacob. They still weren't married, or even engaged, for that matter. Neither thought that marriage could make them any closer than they already were, so they weren't rushing it.

After Charlie handed Mason his plate, she went back to the kitchen. When she was almost there, she shot both Emerson and Mikayla a look that said, "Come on."

The men were too busy watching the football game, and Damian's girlfriend was on her phone, so no one noticed them sneak away. When they got to the kitchen, they saw why Charlie wanted to get them there. On Mikayla's granite counter was a freshly opened bottle of red wine. Emerson opened her mouth to protest, but Charlie held up a finger.